HAUNTED
PET STORIES

HAUNTED PET STORIES

Tales of Ghostly Cats, Spooky Dogs,
and Demonic Bunnies

Retold by Mary Beth Crain

Guilford, Connecticut

Text design: Sheryl P. Kober
Layout: Joanna Beyer
Project editor: Meredith Dias

Library of Congress Cataloging-in-Publication Data

Crain, Mary Beth.
  Haunted pet stories / retold by Mary Beth Crain.
      p. cm.
  ISBN 978-0-7627-6068-8
  1. Animal ghosts. I. Title.
  BF1484.C73 2011
  133.1'4—dc22

                                          2011016297

Printed in the United States of America

10 9 8 7 6 5 4 3 2 1

This book is dedicated to my beloved late husband,
Adam Shields, a great pet lover, and to all my dear
departed cats who so enriched my life. Snicky, Angel,
Rhonda, Petie, White Sox, Trixie, Rex Harrison, Meffie,
Gunsmoke, Godot, Peanut, Blessing, Stockings, Barfie:
Thank you for teaching me the meaning of
unconditional love, the power of which transcends death.

CONTENTS

Contents

INTRODUCTION

Losing a treasured pet is as traumatic as losing any loved one. Only people who have never had a pet or who don't like animals dismiss the human-animal bond as inferior to the human-human bond and consider the idea of a pet going to heaven nothing short of absurd. We animal lovers, however, know better. We know that pets are living beings with unique personalities and abilities just like us, and when they come into our lives, they become members of our families, no less important than their human counterparts.

Unlike their human counterparts, however, animals are experts in the art of unconditional love and naturally exhibit qualities most of us wish we possessed. How many people do you know who would devote themselves entirely to your welfare and happiness, with no thought of their own comfort? Such noble specimens of humanity are few and far between, as anybody who has dated a schmoe or married a creep can attest. When we think of the thoughtless and selfish actions we've committed through the years, of our "just being human"-ness, we should be humbled before our animals and ashamed of our inability to practice the unconditional love that is the ultimate goal of all religions and spiritual practices.

Yes, we humans have to try very hard to feel that kind of love—study, pray, do years of meditation—and even then we fall short of the mark. Yet our pets practice it effortlessly, without thought. It is simply part of their nature. Could that possibly mean that they, and not we, are the most highly evolved of God's creatures?

Do animals engage in torture, crime, and other willful acts of violence against other living beings? Do they dump their newborn babies in garbage cans or leave them locked in cars in hot weather to fry to death while they're having their hair done or doing the grocery shopping? Do they lie and cheat and steal, and break spirits and hearts?

Some humans are incapable of love and loyalty no matter how much love and understanding you give them. But most animals, if you give them love, will remain right there by your side, through thick and thin, forever.

And forever means forever. Death can't sever our bonds with our pets. Even if you don't believe in an afterlife, you can't discount the numerous accounts of paranormal experiences people have had with their departed pets. Our dearly departed animals may appear to us in spirit form or in our dreams and thoughts to assure us of their presence, to guide and guard us, and above all, to comfort us with the knowledge that death is but a mere technicality where love is concerned.

In my own life I've had several paranormal experiences concerning my pets, which I talk about in the chapters "Dreaming of You" and "Reincarnated Pets." They concern two beloved cats: Snicky, who visited me from the astral plane in a dream to comfort me, and Petie, who disappeared and was never seen again, only to return, I'm convinced, in the reincarnated form of a stray kitten two years later.

(By the way, I use "who" rather than "that" when referring to animals. This is technically incorrect, according to the rules of English grammar, which decree that animals don't merit personal pronouns. So you know what you can do with English grammar!)

So when Globe Pequot Press asked me to write this book, I was thrilled because it seemed tailor-made for me. Had I not had a personal encounter with paranormal pets, I might have had a tough time writing a book about pet ghosts. But I'm a believer all the way and so was right at home with the topic.

Haunted Pet Stories is a collection of tales—some the stuff of legend, some genuine eyewitness accounts—about pets and other animals who have transcended death. There are stories about pets who briefly return from the other side and about pets who, like my Snicky, appear in a dream to comfort their owners or to warn them about impending danger. There are stories about pets who suddenly become possessed. There are old stories, like the legend of Molly Leigh, the notorious witch of Burslem, England, and her sinister pet blackbird and the Mauthe Doog, a demonic black canine said to haunt a famous castle on the Isle of Man.

You'll also find amazing accounts of living pets who sense ghostly presences, guardian angels who appear in the unlikely forms of wolves and giant mastiffs, a ghost cat who haunts a famous lighthouse, and even a sprightly pair of haunted leashes!

I hope you find this book to be as much fun to read as it was to write. But it also strikes a serious chord in all of us whose lives have been forever enriched for having had a pet and poorer for having lost one.

In closing, I'd like to share with you a piece I wrote about my dear old cat Rhonda Susan, who passed away in February 2009. I think it expresses the great importance of the human-animal connection and how much our pets give to us, often without our knowing it.

REQUIEM FOR A CAT

A couple of weeks ago, I had to put my oldest cat, Rhonda Susan, to sleep. She was very sick with renal failure and had stopped eating and drinking. Within less than two months, she'd lost so much weight that she looked like a little ghost cat, her shrunken body so light I could pick her up with one hand, her big sea-green eyes enormous in her tiny disappearing face.

As anyone who has had to make this decision knows, it's hell. You feel like you're playing God, without any of the perks. God has the right to giveth life and taketh it away because he created everything to begin with and knows what he's doing. We mere mortals, on the other hand, have a lot of nerve deciding when to pull the plug on another living creature—which is why I prolonged the inevitable until I could no longer bear to see my beloved little girl suffer another day, another hour.

Rhonda would have been seventeen this May. She was born on my bed way back in 1992, in Los Angeles. The runt of the litter, she got her name because she had trouble emerging, and my two friends who were with me started singing that old Beach Boys hit, "Help Me, Rhonda" as we assisted her mother, Angel, in the delivery.

For a while, Rhonda's life hung in the balance. She was so tiny and scrawny that the vet pronounced her not long for this world. Ha! She ended up outliving all my other cats, and in her nearly seventeen years on earth, she survived all manner of traumas and upheavals. One in particular should make the *Cat Guinness Book*.

On a March night in 1999, Rhonda disappeared. I was living in Pasadena at the time, in a neighborhood notorious for roaming coyotes that were decimating the cat population. My friends and I conducted exhaustive searches and posted her picture and description all over the area, but as the days and then weeks passed, hope faded. Finally, I had no choice but to conclude that Rhonda had become another coyote statistic. I mourned her deeply. All I could think about was how she must have died, terrified and alone in the jaws of some hungry beast.

Spring passed into summer, and still I missed my little kitty girl. Then one warm June night, I came home around midnight, and as I parked my convertible on the street in front of my apartment, I thought I heard meowing in the distance. The sound grew closer and louder—escalating to a frantic series of wails that made my heart come to a screeching halt when I saw, halfway down the street, a small gray cat racing toward me. It couldn't be. It couldn't. . . . It was. Rhonda! I ran toward her, and the reunion was like those corny movie scenes of lovers meeting after years of separation. I scooped her up in my arms and burst into sobs, while she meowed for all she was worth and purred like there was a volcano rumbling inside of her, about to explode.

She was half her former size—skin and bones; her fur was matted and flea-ridden. I brought her inside, and she devoured two bowls of food. Then she curled up on my ottoman and basically didn't move from the spot for three weeks. The vet said that she had most likely gotten caught in a basement or garage, and when she'd lost enough weight to fit through a small space, she finally was able to escape. How she ever survived the two-and-a-half months she'd been missing will forever remain a mystery.

Rhonda and I had been through everything together. She endured something like eight moves in her life. She was the only one of my animals left who would remember my late husband, the love of my life, who passed away twelve years ago. She was with him when he died, lying against him in his hospital bed at home. In June of 2006, she came cross-country with me from California to Michigan. Although I had major misgivings about uprooting her from her happy life and subjecting her to such an arduous journey at her age, she was a real trouper and never made a peep the whole 2,200 miles.

But time and miracles finally ran out for Rhonda. At fourteen, her kidneys began to fail. Although she bounced back a few times, she began her final decline a couple of months ago. When she stopped eating and went into the corner of my office closet, huddling next to the heating vent and refusing to respond to me, I knew it was time. I'm sure she knew too. She didn't even resist when I pulled her out from her corner and put her into her carrier.

After examining her, my vet said gently and compassionately, "She's wasting, Mary Beth, and her kidneys have shrunk. I could jump-start her for a few weeks or a month, but it would be prolonging the inevitable. At this point, the kindest and most loving thing would be to end her suffering."

I broke down then, crushing Rhonda to me, and even though her fur was wet with my tears, she never pulled away. As I held her tight, Dr. Troy administered the injection, and within a few seconds her body went limp and she was gone.

I'm still grieving. She was my oldest, dearest companion. I was with her when she took her first breath and when she took her last. Her little kitty bed is still next to the heater in my office, as are her food and water dishes, because as long as they're there, it seems like she'll be coming back to them. At night, when I say goodnight to my Chihuahua, Truman, and my other cat, Junior Augustus, I always add, "Goodnight, Rhonda Susan"—because, who knows, she might be right here beside us in kitty spirit form.

What's really strange is that even though she was such a quiet cat, the house seems so silent and still without her. "It's a measure of how big their spirits are, that they can cause a house to seem so empty by their absence," said a friend of mine who knew and loved her.

I was lucky to have had her, and I was lucky to have had her love me. Goodnight, Rhonda Susan.

Chapter 1

Dead Pets
Society

Can our pets return to us after death? Stories of ghost pets are so common that there's really no question about their existence. But when, where, and why might our dead pets make an appearance? What if we want them to but they don't? Are there ways to contact them? And what's the pet afterlife like?

One of the incontestable authorities on pets and the afterlife was the late Harold Sharp. A respected British medium and author of the fascinating little book, *Animals in the Spirit World,* Sharp was something of a shaman, passing effortlessly back and forth between the dimensions of earth and spirit. He was as at home on the astral plane as he was in his London flat.

"Since there is no death to any form of life," wrote Sharp, "your animal friends live on as surely as do your human friends."

Because animals can see auras—the energy fields radiating from every living thing—they also will be attracted to the auras of their owners, whether on this plane or the next. Sharp maintained that when our pets die they go to a blissful realm where they are able to remain in contact with us by way of our distinct auras. The aura of an animal lover, he noted, emits an "orange radiance" to which animals, alive or dead, instantly respond.

"We want you who love animals, or who have lost some pet dear to you, to realise that they still live, happy and carefree, in a most wonderful realm. I want you to realise too that every time you think or speak of them, it is as though through your orange ray you called 'Come.' And they do come. Do not let them find you sad, for that would make them feel sad, too."

During his many mediumistic adventures, Sharp often saw or received messages from dearly departed pets. On one occasion, he was visiting an elderly woman named Sarah Chester, who was bedridden with arthritis, and they were discussing what happens after death. Mrs. Chester remarked, "Well, you know, I never could swallow the usual idea of heaven—golden floors and pearly gates and all that sort of thing. It always seemed very far-fetched to me. If I can have my old Jumbo there, I shall be perfectly happy. That will be heaven."

Jumbo was Sarah Chester's faithful old shepherd—her constant companion for many years who had never left her side during her six years of paralysis. When he died, soon after Sharp's last visit with her, Sarah followed him within a few months.

Sometime afterward, Sharp said, he had a sitting with the well-known London medium, Mrs. Neville. During the course of their session, Mrs. Neville announced, "There is a woman here, about sixty years of age. She is saying 'Chester.' That is probably her name or the name of the town where she lived. She has a big shaggy dog with her; she calls him Jumbo. She is dressed in tweeds and is just off for a walk with the dog. My word, they are an energetic pair!"

"How wonderful!" wrote Sharp. "How pleasing. It was most surely my old friend with her old companion. The other world is indeed a painless zone where distress and sorrow are unknown. Sarah Chester's paralysis is a thing of the past. And the stiffened old age of Jumbo is also a thing forgotten."

Another experience, even more fantastic, involved a dog from Sharp's own childhood.

"When I was six years old, we had a big, lumbering dog named Hector. He knocked me over many times and then would tug at my jacket, trying to pull me up again," Sharp wrote.

"No dog drank as much as Hector. If he had been a man instead of a dog, I fear he might well have become a drunkard. I never knew a dog with such a thirst. He gulped down every bucket of water, puddle of water, the water in the horses' drinking troughs. . . . If none of these was available, he would pull at my mother's skirt and draw her towards the pump."

One evening, many years after Hector had passed on, Sharp was attending a spiritualist circle at the home of a Glover Botham in Golders Green when, in full view of everyone, Hector suddenly materialized.

"Hector had been dead for twenty years," Sharp observed. "I had almost forgotten his existence. There was a large blue china bowl of water on the floor in the center of the circle, as this is thought sometimes to add power to aid the various manifestations. Hector forthwith set to and very noisily lapped up the whole of it. Then he barked loudly and slowly disappeared."

You might be tempted to dismiss the incident as a figment of Sharp's imagination, except that it was corroborated by Glover Botham and others at the circle as well as by two ladies in the next-door flat who ran into Botham the next day and mentioned they'd heard barking coming from his home the previous evening. "We didn't know you had a dog," they remarked.

Pet psychics are, of course, numerous, and while some might be suspect, many are quite reputable and have located missing animals, read the minds of living pets, and communicated with those who have crossed over.

A pet psychic in New York City says she reads energy auras like the ones Harold Sharp describes. She refers to this as "photo sensing."

"Dates appear above the animal's head, and the picture begins to move like in a movie," she explained. "I can see the buildings, clothing, and surroundings related to the past life."

A *Newsweek* article about the booming pet psychic biz cited the example of Dr. Andrea Chen, a New Jersey veterinarian, who wasn't a believer until she met pet psychic Shira Plotzker at a pet expo. Without being asked, Plotzker suddenly exclaimed, "I'm going into psychic mode!"

"It was about my horse," recalled Chen. "She said that my horse was coming through, my horse who had passed away. And that he thanked me for being who I was and how I treated him, and that there was nothing that I could have done, and it was the tumor he had in his head. And I thought, huh. She couldn't have known that."

Chen experienced a great sense of relief and closure. "I cried," she admitted. "But something like this is reassurance for the owner that they're doing the right thing."

⊹

Let's say you don't want to pay those stiff pet psychic rates. Is there a do-it-yourself way to contact your departed pet? Absolutely.

According to Joshua Warren, author of *Pet Ghosts: Animal Encounters from Beyond the Grave,* there's nothing terribly complicated about communicating with the dead. Here are some of his recommendations:

1. Keep your pet's things in their familiar spots. "Don't forget them because they're gone," says Warren. Toys, blankets, and food bowls are happy reminders for your spirit friend—and "the ghosts will go where they're happiest."

2. Create optimum conditions for spirit contact. "Lower the humidity, turn off the TV, and stay away from appliances," Warren instructs. "You want to minimize the possibility of other energies intruding and mixing up signals." By all means, turn off the light, as "a luminous form is easier to see in the dark."

3. Get a fluorescent lightbulb, which can detect a charge, or a strobe light, which "operates similar to a camera shutter," notes Warren. "It freezes that motion moving too fast for your brain to perceive."

4. If you think you see your pet, rule out the obvious before getting all excited. Make sure it's not the shadow of another object or your mind playing tricks on you. Once a valid manifestation is established, says Warren, you can fully interact with your pet as you did in life, for as long as the environmental conditions permit.

5. Finally, keep an open mind. "If a person desires the spirit to stay, vocalizes that wish, and reinforces it on a daily basis, the ghost can remain indefinitely," Warren assures us.

✛

As I mentioned in the introduction, I lost my dear old cat, Rhonda Susan, a few years ago, when she passed on of kidney failure. For at least a year, I couldn't even think of putting away her things. I left her water bowl and her "sleeping towel" on the floor of my office closet because as long as they were there, it seemed as if she was, too. I talked to her every day and told her how much I loved her and missed her. I cried a lot.

As badly as I wanted to, I never saw Rhonda's ghost. But I believe her brothers, Junior Augustus, the cat, and Truman, the Chihuahua, most certainly did. They would often stare intently at the corner of the closet where she liked to sleep and eat, eyes fixed on some invisible entity, tails up. More than once I found Junior on his big sister's towel, jumping around as if playing with her as he used to do. Truman would go over to the area, tail wagging, and growl softly, and a number of times when Truman was lying on my bed, he would jump up, stare at the doorway, and begin to bark excitedly at something only he could see.

Even though Rhonda has yet to materialize to me, I feel comforted by these occurrences, and I continue to hope that someday my dainty, tortoiseshell tabby girl will appear to me once more, jumping up on my lap, purring her "big purr," and butting her little head against my arm. Meanwhile, I take heart from Sharp's words: "Your pet is happy now in the fields and lanes of Heaven, which is like life on earth, only lovelier and more peaceful."

Chapter 2

The Ghost Cat's
Final Request

They say that human ghosts often hang around on the earth plane when they have unfinished business. Animal ghosts are apparently no different. In this story, based on a true incident, a dead cat came back to his young owner and refused to leave until certain conditions had been met.

Ellie Thurlow was eight when she got her first pet: an adorable kitten who followed her everywhere. The kitten was black with four white paws and a little white dinner napkin. Ellie named him Tux—short for Tuxedo—and reveled in her new role as kitty mama.

When you're eight and everybody's telling you what to do, it's a big step up to be in charge and to have someone dependent on you for a change. Yes, *someone:* to Ellie, Tux was, for all intents and purposes, her child, her playmate, and her best friend. He might as well have been human. No—he was better than human, because Ellie could always count on his devotion, no matter what.

Ellie had gotten Tux from her second-grade teacher, Mrs. Rath. The little thing had been hanging around the school, thin and hungry, and Mrs. Rath, the nicest and prettiest second-grade teacher in the world, took it home.

A week later, at recess, Mrs. Rath called Ellie over to her. Smiling, she said, "Ellie, how would you like a kitten?"

"A kitten?" Ellie was thoroughly surprised. "You mean the little black-and-white one you took home?"

"That's right."

"But why? Don't you like him?"

"Oh, I love him," Mrs. Rath assured her. "But I'm afraid my two dogs don't. They simply won't accept the little fellow. Jealous, you know?"

Ellie nodded. She could relate. She remembered how she'd felt when Mom and Dad brought home the new baby. After a few days of being ignored, all she wanted was to have her tiny rival disappear forever.

"I don't know, Mrs. Rath. We've already got two cats. They might not like him either."

"I see," Mrs. Rath nodded and pinched Ellie's round, rosy cheek. "Well, I'm sure I'll find him a home somewhere."

"Mrs. Rath?" Ellie looked up at her teacher.

"Yes, dear?"

"How come you asked me? I mean, instead of one of the other kids?"

"Oh, I don't know," Mrs. Rath smiled down at her. Ellie loved Mrs. Rath's smile; it was warm and bright and made her feel like the sun was washing over her, even on a rainy day. "I suppose it's because you love animals so much, as much as I do. You're always reading about them and drawing them, and I saw you feeding the kitten one day from your lunch and talking to him as though he were one of your friends."

"I know!" Ellie giggled. "He kind of felt like my friend. He seemed to understand me."

"Well, run along now or you'll miss recess," Mrs. Rath playfully pulled one of Ellie's pigtails. "And don't worry, Ellie—someone will take the kitty."

That night at dinner Ellie told her parents about her conversation with Mrs. Rath. "Do you think we could take the kitten?" she asked.

"I don't know, honey," her mother said. "What about Minnie and Ginny?"

"Well, we could try," Ellie pleaded. "Maybe they'll get along."

"If you really want this kitten, you'll have to take care of it," her father gave her one of his "and I mean it!" looks. "It'll be yours."

"Oh, I will, I will!" Ellie clapped her hands. Her very own kitten!

The next day Ellie ran like the wind to school and breathlessly told Mrs. Rath the good news. At lunch, Mrs. Rath went home and got the kitten and brought it into the classroom in its little carrier. Ellie and her new charge were the center of attention for the rest of the day.

"Have you thought of a name for him?" Mrs. Rath asked.

"Tux," Ellie promptly replied. "Because he looks like he's wearing a tuxedo."

"He's a tuxedo cat, all right," laughed Mrs. Rath.

The unusual thing about Tux was his eyes—one was green, the other was gold. They shone like gems: emerald and topaz.

"Why are his eyes different colors?" Ellie asked Mrs. Rath.

"Because God decided he was special," Mrs. Rath smiled her golden smile.

From the very first, Ellie and Tux were inseparable, and they played together indoors and out. More like a dog than a cat, Tux went on walks with his mistress and turned out to be a fine retriever, fetching small objects that Ellie threw and returning them to her with lightning speed.

At first the older cats, Minnie and Ginny, were not happy with the usurper to the throne. They hissed at Tux and swatted at him, and Ellie was terrified they might kill the beleaguered little fellow. But Tux humbled himself before the royal tyrants, and after a few days they were satisfied that he understood his place in the pecking order.

Everyone in the family loved Tux except for Grandpa Thurlow. Grandpa was a crusty old man, tough and unsentimental. He didn't go much for pets, which he considered to be a nuisance, and he declared that the only animal fit to have around was a good coon dog.

He hated cats. Even the barn cats, which were so useful for killing mice and other vermin, did not impress him. Whenever Grandpa came to visit, the two older cats steered clear of him. But little Tux, to whom everybody was a friend, went right over to him and rubbed against his leg.

"Git!" snarled Grandpa, pushing Tux away with his foot.

"Don't kick him, Grandpa!" Ellie yelled.

"I ain't kickin' him! I'm just movin' him," grunted Grandpa. "But if he don't hightail it, he'll git a kick for sure."

From then on, whenever Grandpa came over, Tux was confined to the bedroom.

All cats have their favorite spots, some stranger than others. Tux's favorite spot was the cedar chest at the foot of Ellie's bed. He loved to sleep on it, and if it was open, he'd jump in and explore its fragrant depths. Ellie had to be careful to make sure Tux was outside the chest before she closed the lid, because one time the curious kitten had gotten into the chest and fallen asleep, hidden in some pillows, and Ellie had closed it up without seeing him. He was trapped for hours, until her mother happened to walk by Ellie's bedroom and heard his muffled meows and desperate clawing.

A year went by. Tux grew into a beautiful cat, long and lean. People remarked on how handsome he was, and Ellie beamed with pride. Then, one terrible day, Ellie's world collapsed. She'd just come in from school and was headed toward the kitchen for her usual cookies and milk, when her mother stopped her.

"Ellie, honey, sit down."

"Why, Mom?"

"Because I've got some bad news."

Ellie's heart began to pound. She'd never seen that look on her mother's face—a look of sadness, compassion, and fear, all rolled into one.

"What bad news?" Ellie remained standing. She couldn't move.

"It's Tux, honey. Grandpa found him dead in the road."

Ellie sat down. "Where?" she whispered.

"Down by the old creamery, at the foot of Hobb's Hill."

Ellie began to cry. "He can't be dead. He can't!" she kept repeating. Then she said, "Where is he now?"

"Grandpa threw him over the hill."

"No!" Ellie screamed. "I'm going to look for him."

"No, Ellie," her mother said firmly. "It's best to leave things as they are. You'd never find him, anyway."

Ellie was heartbroken. How could her grandfather have been so callous as to toss her beloved cat to the wind like a bag of trash? Why couldn't he have brought Tux back, so she could at least have given him a dignified funeral?

A week went by. The sun had gone down upon Ellie's life. Not even Mrs. Rath's smile could bring it back.

Then, one afternoon when Ellie was in her bedroom doing her homework, she heard a scratching noise coming from her cedar chest. She shivered. What if it were a mouse?

She hated mice. Trembling, she slowly lifted the lid. And there, sitting on a pillow, was Tux. He jumped out of the chest and onto the bed. Ellie just stared at him. It couldn't be. It had to be another cat who looked identical to Tux and had somehow gotten into the house.

Then she looked at the cat's eyes, gleaming like gems— emerald and topaz.

"Tux!" she cried. "You didn't die! It wasn't you!"

Tux just sat there, purring. Then he meowed softly.

Ellie ran to get her mother. "Mom!" she screamed. "Tux is here! In my room!"

"What?" Mrs. Thurlow gasped.

"Come see!"

Ellie grabbed her mother's hand and dragged her to her bedroom. But Tux wasn't there.

"He's here somewhere, Mom," Ellie insisted. "He was right here on the bed, purring like he always does."

"Sweetheart, I think you imagined him," Mrs. Thurlow said gently. "You want him back so much that you thought he was here."

"No!" Ellie cried. "He was here! I swear it!" She searched the room frantically, looking under the bed, in the closet, behind the dresser. But Tux was nowhere to be found. Falling onto her bed, Ellie sobbed herself to sleep.

She was awakened by the sound of purring and the feeling of a tiny wet nose on her cheek. Tux. She reached out and touched him. He felt solid, real. His purring grew louder, and he pawed at her cheek. He seemed to be trying to tell her something.

"What is it, Tux?" she whispered.

But Tux could only purr and rub against her.

Ellie decided that Tux had returned because he missed her so much. No one else could see him, but that was okay. Ghost or not, she had him back.

The days went by, and Tux stayed in Ellie's bedroom. Although Ellie was happy, Tux seemed restless and kept trying to get her attention. She tried to figure out what he wanted. Then, one night it hit her. He wanted a proper burial!

"Is that it, Tux?" she whispered. "Is that what you want?"

Tux purred as though he would burst and bumped his head against her again and again.

The next morning, Ellie rose early and stole out of the house, spade in one hand, cardboard shoebox in the other. She went to Hobb's Hill and scoured the area until she found the remains of a black-and-white tuxedo cat with sightless eyes of emerald and topaz. Tenderly, she placed the body in the shoebox. Then, she dug a small grave and buried her best friend.

Tux never reappeared, and Ellie was satisfied that his final request had been granted.

Chapter 3

When Ghost Cats
Come to Visit

During my research for Haunted Pet Stories, *I came across count-less accounts of pets who have appeared to their owners after death. For some unknown reason, however, there seemed to be a preponderance of ghost cat stories, with common themes. Own-ers would hear familiar kitty footsteps and purring, or they might feel the cat's presence, often in bed. Sometimes the animal would be visible and seemingly solid. Were these dead pets stopping by just to visit? Were they coming to provide comfort and reassurance to their grieving owners? Or were they there to warn of impending danger—or death?*

Not long ago, I came across a fascinating online post detail-ing a genuine phantom cat experience. The woman who wrote it was an admitted ailurophile (cat lover) who wrote that she particularly liked when her cats climbed on her bed and kneaded the blankets with their paws.

"A few years ago, I was experiencing this same sensation while lying in bed," she wrote. "Though we do have a cat, I knew it wasn't him because we have been keeping him in the basement since my son started crawling and then walk-ing three and a half years ago," she wrote.

The woman also noticed that no sound accompanied the kneading. Usually, a cat will purr loudly as it engages in this activity, a throwback from early childhood when kittens push on the mother's belly to stimulate the milk glands as they're feeding. Although she couldn't see or hear the cat, the sensation of a small four-legged animal walking on the bed and pushing on the covers was unmistakable.

The ghost cat visited for several months, each time silently kneading the bedcovers. Then the bedtime activity suddenly stopped. The woman was relieved, as she was already sleep-deprived from dealing with a toddler who was up a good part of the night.

One morning, she was trying to sleep when she felt something in bed with her.

"My son gets up early these days and watches his cartoons while I try and sleep," she wrote. "This morning, like all mornings, he was in and out of my room with questions and things he wanted to tell me. As much as I wanted to sleep, I was wide awake instead.

"I was lying there waiting for another interruption when I began to feel a light walking on my bed. At first I thought it was just my son trying to sneak up on me, but then I heard him laughing in the living room. Confused, I sat up and looked down at my legs, fully expecting to see our new kitten. But there was nothing on my bed.

"After I got up, I was able to confirm that both our grown cat and our new kitten were still in the basement. My son had not let either of them up.

"So now I apparently have a phantom cat to join my two living cats. At least I don't have to feed this one!"

This story is somewhat unusual, in that the ghost cat was unknown to its host. Generally, such an animal is a former family member, returning to its familiar stomping grounds. Perhaps this phantom visitor had lived in the house long ago, or maybe it was just lost and lonely for human companionship.

✛

Another ghost cat story concerns a young woman, Jennifer, who was very attached to her stepfather's cat, a big, orange-brown lover boy named Marmalade. Shortly after the family had moved into an old country house in Virginia, Jennifer went to visit her father and brother in Florida for a few months. One night she thought she saw Marmalade run past her bed.

"I knew that was impossible," she said. "After all, Marmalade was five hundred miles away. I decided I'd just been dreaming. But I sure missed him and couldn't wait to get back to him."

The next day her mother phoned her. "Jen, I've got sad news," she said. "Marmalade died last night in your room."

Although devastated by the loss, Jennifer took comfort in the knowledge that her beloved cat had paid her a visit from the beyond and that his spirit would always be close by.

After Jennifer returned home, the visits continued.

"I kept seeing him every so often, running past me," she recalled. "We have two other cats, Jack and Mack, but it wasn't either of them. Marmalade always had this habit of running by you, stopping and falling over, inviting you to bend down and rub his tummy. It seems like he's still running, but he doesn't do the stopping and falling now. Just races by and disappears."

Jennifer was unsure what to do. Was her poor cat earthbound and trying to get over to the other side? Should she contact a pet psychic and try to send Marmalade into the light? Or should she just let her faithful pet remain with her in spirit?

She decided to let Marmalade hang around.

"I do love that cat to death" . . . and beyond.

✛

Laura's story, which took place when she was a child, is similarly eerie.

"One night as I was getting ready to drift off to sleep, I felt a kind of heavy presence pressing into my back," she recounted. "It was warm and felt like a cat curled up on me. But my cat was an outside cat and was nowhere near me at the time.

"I would get up, walk around, and lie down again, and without fail, the pressure would come back. Needless to say, I was creeped out but not at all scared, as the presence was more of a comforting nature. Finally, I fell asleep, with the 'thing' still lying on me.

"The next morning as I walked to the bus stop for school, I found my cat dead in the road. She had been hit by a car. Of course, I was quite spooked. That feeling never came back after that one night."

✛

Then there was Brutus, whose owner, Renee, got quite a shock one night when he paid her a call from the spirit world.

"About five years ago, my lovely cat, Brutus, was run over by a car and killed. I was heartbroken, as was my other cat, Les," Renee said. "Three weeks later, I was lying in bed one morning, listening to my son getting ready for work—so I know I wasn't dreaming—when a cat jumped from the floor onto my chest and then walked onto the bed beside me. It felt too light to be Les, who's a big boy.

"Not ten seconds later, Les jumped up onto my bedside table and walked over my chest. I realized that the other cat had to be Brutus, since Les never jumped from the floor, because of his weight. It was Brutus who always jumped onto my chest. Also, Brutus was a hunter who liked to roam around at night. But he always came in when my son went to work and came straight to my room."

Renee was shocked by the experience. But she was even more astonished a few days later when she awoke and leaned out of bed to get her slippers.

"There was Brutus, sitting under my bedside table. He looked totally solid," she recalled. "He was a beautiful, gray and white, long-haired cat, and I never imagined that he could have been any more beautiful than he was in life. But now he emanated an incredible kind of radiance, and love seemed to be shining from his eyes."

Even though Renee was thrilled to see Brutus, she knew he needed to find his new home in the spirit world.

"I sat there a long time, talking to him and telling him that I loved him but that it was time to go home. Then I closed my eyes and prayed for Brutus to find peace. When I opened my eyes, he was gone."

Les never recovered from the death of his brother. He remained depressed, and three years later, at the age of sixteen, he grew very ill.

"As I held him in my arms in his last moments," said Renee, "I said to him, 'It's time to go home, Les. Brutus is waiting for you.' As soon as I said Brutus's name, Les turned his head toward my hand and licked it gently. Then he closed his eyes and was gone."

✛

Sometimes, when a person is about to die, a pet who has crossed over will appear to alert the person of her or his approaching death or to welcome them into the next life. Such, apparently, was the case with Dottie Rehnquist.

Dottie was a great animal lover who had never been without a cat or dog and usually had several of each. One pet, in particular, was close to her heart—a big, tawny Labrador named Elsie who seemed to be more human than dog and who knew Dottie's soul.

Dottie and Elsie shared such a special bond that they communicated telepathically, as if each knew what the other was thinking.

"I had had many dear pets through the years," Dottie commented. "But none with whom I was as close as Elsie. I almost believed in reincarnation, for she was like a loved one from a past life."

When Elsie passed on, Dottie mourned her deeply. There were no words to describe her sense of loss, and there seemed to be no end to her grief. While in the past, she had always eventually taken in another stray when one of her pets passed on, after Elsie's death she never got another dog. She couldn't bear the thought of any other creature replacing Elsie.

Ten years went by. Then one day, her daughter Sally received a letter from Dottie, telling of an amazing experience.

"Mom said she was sitting in her favorite chair, watching TV, when out of nowhere Elsie appeared in front of her," Sally recalled. "Of course, she couldn't believe her eyes. The most astonishing thing was that Elsie looked wonderful, perfectly healthy and happy. Mom reached out to her, and Elsie got up on her hind legs and put her paws on her face, licking her ecstatically. Then she vanished.

"Because they had always had this telepathic connection, Mom knew why Elsie had come to her. 'I believe I'll be crossing over soon,' she wrote. 'I just have a feeling that's what Elsie came to tell me.'"

Sally was dumbfounded. As far as she knew, her mother was in good health. Nonetheless, she immediately made plans to visit her. She hadn't been with her a week when Dottie died of a sudden heart attack.

Elsie had been a heavenly messenger, and in the midst of her grief, Sally found comfort in the certainty that the gentle Lab and her mother were together once more, this time forever.

One cat enthusiast who calls himself Crazy Johnny has many a ghost-cat tale to tell. "I have as many cat ghosts as I've had cats," he bragged in his blog, The Pride. "And you know how many that is!"

"The night my mother's dear Theresa, our first bottle-fed kitten, passed away, I heard her footsteps plunkety plunk plunking down the stairs beside me, like she always did. Clear as a bell. Except no cat was there. That was at my mother's house. The same night, at home in my apartment, I felt a cat jump onto my bed and walk the length from foot to head only to disappear at the pillow. No cat can have been there because the door was closed."

Johnny's cat Moby frequently visits from the spirit realm. "Many times since Moby passed, I have heard him crossing the living room toward his bed, his distinctive quick, sharp feet hurrying along, and rustling around in the bed before settling down to nap."

In addition to his own ghost cats, Johnny has been visited by a strange phantom feline. "I frequently see the ghost of a cat in the apartment that's not one of mine at all—a large, dark-colored male who walks in and out of the door at will. I have often seen him coming down my short entrance hall, a sort of smoky, dark film in a cat shape. I have also seen him jumping on the living room windowsill, in the kitchen circling the leg of the chair as if waiting for his dinner, and once found him playing in the tub before he vanished."

When Johnny asked the building manager if another cat had ever lived in his apartment, the man replied that the former tenant had had a large tabby male.

Ghost-cat sightings apparently run in the family. "Aunt Betty tells of the night she was awakened suddenly from a deep sleep to see Catherine, her gorgeous all-white cat, sitting on the edge of the dresser, staring down at her and watching her sleep with her piercing gold eyes. This, of course, could not be. Ms. Catherine had passed away the day before. Aunt Betty sat up and turned on the light. There was no Catherine. There was no cat at all."

It was the famous French avant-garde playwright Jean Cocteau who remarked, "I love cats because I love my home, and after a while they become its visible soul." And perhaps, after a while, its invisible soul as well.

Chapter 4
The Ghost Cat of
Fairport Harbor

*The legendary lighthouse in Fairport Harbor, Ohio, is famous for a
ghost cat who has haunted the premises for at least a century, and
whose presence was verified in 2001, when a worker made a grue-
some discovery. The cat had belonged to a woman who had lost
her little boy to diphtheria and whose cats, given to her by her husband after the child's tragic demise, were her only source of comfort until her own death not long afterward. The "Gray Ghost," as it
was nicknamed, is quite playful, and apparently has no intention
of going into the light anytime soon.*

The historic Fairport Harbor Lighthouse—located on the
eastern shore of Lake Erie at the mouth of the Grand River—
is famous not only for guiding ships for more than a century but also for providing a safe haven for slaves making
their way to freedom along the Underground Railroad. But
its chief attraction today is a phantom cat who has haunted
the lighthouse for years.

The cat is believed to have belonged to Mary Babcock,
wife of Captain Joseph Babcock, the lighthouse's head
keeper some 140 years ago. A Civil War veteran, Captain Babcock succeeded the first keeper, Samuel Butler, who held the
post from 1825 until 1871, when the lighthouse was rebuilt.
Captain and Mrs. Babcock resided in the second-floor quarters of the keeper's house with their children, two of whom,
Hattie and Robbie, were born in the house. The Babcock

family kept the lighthouse for over half a century. Joseph's eldest son, Daniel, was the assistant lighthouse-keeper from 1901 to 1919 and head keeper until the lighthouse's 1922 decommissioning.

Then, for more than twenty years, the keeper's house sat vacant and the lighthouse unused until the citizens of Fairport Harbor banded together to save them from demolition. Eventually, the two structures were turned into a museum devoted to nautical and historic exhibits pertaining to the local region and operated by a newly formed historical society.

In 1989, museum curator Pam Brent, who lived in the Babcock's old second-floor quarters, reported seeing a gray ghost cat cavorting around the keeper's house and lighthouse.

"It would skitter across the floor near the kitchen, like it was playing," Brent said. "I would catch glimpses of it from time to time. Then, one evening, I felt its presence when it jumped on the bed, and I felt its weight pressing on me. At first, it kind of freaked me out. But ghosts don't bother me. They are part of the world."

Soon other society members working in and around the site were seeing the mystery feline, and visitors began attesting to having seen "small puffs of gray smoke" in the ghostly shape of a cat dashing by them and disappearing just as fast.

The ghost cat became a local legend, drawing many visitors to the "haunted lighthouse." Then, in 2001, while upgrading the heating, ventilation, and air-conditioning system of the keeper's house, a worker named Bryan Smith made a horrific discovery that elevated the ghost cat of the old Fairport Harbor Lighthouse to a whole new status.

"We were installing the new system in the basement, and I was working my way into a tight crawl space," Smith recalled. "I looked to my right and there, next to my head, were the mummified remains of a gray cat."

The historical society knew a good public relations opportunity when it saw one. They promptly put the mummified cat on display inside the museum, where today it rests stiff but peaceful inside a glass case and is the museum's main draw. People come from far and wide to gaze upon its macabre form, which has been described by one visitor as "very creepy, like an Egyptian mummy without the wrappings."

Further research suggested the cat's identity. When Robbie Babcock was five years old, he came down with one of the most dreaded diseases of the time, diphtheria. Utterly helpless, his devastated parents watched him die, and Mary Babcock never recovered from the shock and grief. She sank into a deep depression and took to her bed, where she remained until her own death a few years later.

To cheer up his wife, Joseph Babcock gave her cats, which kept her company and whose crazy antics made her laugh. Mary's favorite feline was a spunky gray ball of mischief who loved to roll about on the bed and pounce on her feet and hands under the coverlet. This cat was famous for its wild bursts of energy, and would often dash around the house, whizzing by the other occupants in a frenzy of playfulness.

After Mary Babcock's death, the other cats disappeared. But the gray cat remained on the premises for years, until it, too, eventually disappeared . . . or so they thought.

Today, even though its mummified body attests to its demise, the ghost of Mary Babcock's precocious gray cat is as active and playful as ever—and shows no inclination to leave. It's apparently perfectly comfortable in its old surroundings. There is, however, another ghost who is not so content: Robbie Babcock. Museum volunteers believe that the spirit of the dead boy haunts the downstairs of the building. Unfortunately, unlike the ghost cat, Robbie is neither happy nor playful. Those who have encountered him describe "a presence of dread," sometimes accompanied by cold air and a foul, decaying odor.

Robbie isn't the only human ghost hanging around the Fairport Harbor Lighthouse, either. Armed with special equipment, the Scientific Investigative Ghost Hunting Team (S.I.G.H.T.) was able to make some "ghost box" (a special AM/FM radio used by paranormal investigators) recordings in the lighthouse tower and the keeper's house. In the upstairs bedroom that had been Mary Babcock's, the team asked the question, "Is there a Captain Babcock here?" When they played back the recording, a "weird-sounding" voice seemed to be saying, "Babcock." To the inquiry, "Are there any ghosts here?" the same voice replied, "Spirit of Babcock."

Near the top of the lighthouse, the investigators got some unexpected information regarding Captain Butler, the first head keeper. When the team played back the ghost box recording, they heard a muffled, crackled response of one word, "Spirit," to the question, "Where's Captain Butler?"

Another team of paranormal sleuths, the Ohio Researchers of Banded Spirits (O.R.B.S.), captured the sound of a cat meowing during an overnight investigation of the lighthouse. No cats were on the premises at the time.

✛

The majority of ghost pet "hauntings" are temporary visitations to the pet's human family. The pet usually returns for a brief period immediately or shortly after expiring either to let its owner know it is okay, to check on its family, or to warn of or circumvent danger. That said, many places seem to attract permanent cat spirits.

For example, there is the famous Demon Cat Ghost of Capitol Hill—a strange, shadowy black cat known as D.C. who allegedly haunts various buildings in Washington, D.C., from the U.S. Capitol Building to the White House, the National Mall, and the Watergate Hotel. D.C.'s home base appears to be the Capitol's basement, an eerie vault that happens to be where the catafalque, a raised platform for the caskets of those who are given state funerals, is stored. In the 1800s, when the city was battling a rat infestation, many cats were brought into the basement of the Capitol building, and D.C. may have been one of those who simply never left.

Ghost cats apparently haunt the Russian capital of Moscow, as well. On the city's major thoroughfare, Tverskaya Street, residents swear that a black cat haunts the area, appearing at the stroke of midnight, walking around, and then disappearing. It has acquired such celebrity that it's cited in *Britain's Encyclopaedia of Ghosts and Spirits*. Nearby, a whole family of ghost cats is said to haunt the Novokuznetskaya metro station, where there have been multiple sightings of phantom cats and kittens.

Redlands, California, might be a far cry from Moscow and Washington, DC, but it, too, seems to be a stomping ground for ghost cats. In the city's fashionable old neighborhood, there was once an imposing Victorian mansion whose owner, an eccentric spinster, had an avid obsession with little dogs and an equally passionate aversion to cats. At one time, locals say, she had over forty Chihuahuas, Pomeranians, papillons, and dachshunds. The mad old biddy is also rumored to have poisoned any unlucky feline who roamed her property.

Today, the manse is long gone, but many people have reported seeing a ghost cat prowling the property and walking back and forth up a staircase that leads to nowhere. The cat has a disturbing distinguishing feature: It is headless.

Two other famous Redlands ghost cats, Boots and Peach, died years ago and now live outside Rama Garden, an exclusive Thai restaurant. A number of the establishment's patrons, and practically all the employees, have seen the phantom felines. Rama Garden is notoriously cat-friendly, which is undoubtedly why Boots and Peach hang around. After all, once you've found heaven on earth, why leave—even if you're dead?

Chapter 5

A Ghost and His Dog

Some of the strangest animal ghost stories seem to come from England. Perhaps that's because the English are so used to ghosts, their history being permeated by them, and also because London is the birthplace of the Society for Psychical Research (SPR), an organization established in 1882 for legitimate study of the paranormal. The following case study, adapted from Elliott O'Donnell's The Screaming Skull and Other Ghost Stories, *is one of the more unusual tales from the SPR files, because it concerns not only a belligerent human ghost but also his equally belligerent ghost dog.*

One winter night in 1894, James Durham, a railroad station watchman in the town of Darlington, England, was on duty when he felt the need to take a break. Cold and hungry, he decided to go down to the porter's cellar, where there was a comfortable gas fire, to get a bite to eat.

Durham had taken off his heavy coat and was warming himself by the fire when a strange man walked into the cellar from an adjoining room, followed by a big black dog.

"As soon as he entered, my eye was upon him and his eye was upon me," Durham stated in a letter he later sent to the Society for Psychical Research. "We were intently watching each other as he moved on to the front of the fire."

Durham noticed that the man's attire seemed out of place; he was wearing an old-fashioned cutaway coat with gilt buttons and a Scotch cap. The watchman asked the stranger his name. The man did not reply; instead, he smiled an odd smile. Then, the next thing Durham knew, the man struck him . . . or rather, seemed to. Although Durham saw a hand come at him, he didn't feel the blow.

"I up with my fist and struck back at him," Durham recounted. But his fist seemed to go right through his assailant, striking against the stone above the fireplace and badly skinning his knuckles. "The man seemed to be struck back into the fire and uttered a strange, unearthly squeak," noted Durham.

At the same moment, the dog lunged at Durham, sinking his teeth into Durham's calf. Yet, the bite didn't hurt. . . or did it? The watchman felt what might be described as phantom pain, the kind an amputee feels in the place where his limb once was.

By then, the stranger had gotten back on his feet. He clicked his tongue, and the dog backed off and then followed his master back into the adjoining room.

Durham immediately lit his lantern and checked the adjoining room. But, in his words, "there was neither dog nor man, and no outlet for them except the one by which they had entered."

Convinced he'd encountered a ghost and understandably shaken, Durham described the incident to his fellow workmen. They might have laughed it off, except for two things: One, Durham was known for his reliability and honesty, and he was neither a drinker nor a practical joker; when he said something, you could count on its veracity. Two, there was history to back up the watchman's story. Years before, a clerk at the Darlington station by the name of Winter had shot himself, and his body had been taken to the exact spot where Durham had encountered the ghost. Durham had never heard of Winter and was unaware of any suicides on the premises.

An aging station veteran known as Old Edward Pease, "father of railways," was particularly interested in Durham's story. He grilled the watchman. "Are you sure you hadn't fallen asleep and dreamed the whole thing?" "Had you taken a snifter or two?"

"I had not been a minute in the cellar, and was just going to get something to eat," Durham assured Pease. "I was certainly not under the influence of strong drink. I have always been a nondrinker. My mind at the time was entirely free of trouble."

It was then that Pease and other longtime employees of the Darlington station told Durham about Winter. "They told me my description exactly corresponded to his appearance and the way he dressed, and also that he had a black retriever just like the one which gripped me."

There were no marks on Durham to attest either to being struck or bitten. But the knuckles of his right hand were raw and bruised.

The incident went down in the SPR files as "The Battle with the Ghost," a genuinely paranormal event distinguished by its uncharacteristic violence. As one investigator wrote, "It is the only instance which I remember in which an apparition attempted to injure, and even in this solitary instance there was no real harm done."

"The Battle with the Ghost" proves beyond a doubt that a faithful dog will follow his master anywhere—even beyond the grave.

Chapter 6
The Haunted Horses

When it comes to tales of animal hauntings, the story of Jacques L'Esperance and his two magical—but cursed—black horses is right up there with the best. The time was the early nineteenth century; the place was Grosse Pointe Woods, Michigan, a pious rural community that suddenly found itself under siege from none other than the devil himself, who was determined to claim Jacques' magnificent steeds for himself, no matter what. The following version of the story is adapted from S.E. Schlosser's Spooky Michigan.

It was with great pride in both his purchase and his good horse sense that Jacques L'Esperance led his two new stallions into his stable the evening of his return from a trip to Chicago. A well-to-do farmer, Jacques was famed far and wide for his horse stable, the finest in all of Grosse Pointe Woods and beyond. Although he was familiar with all manner and breed of horses, even he had never seen the likes of this magnificent pair of equine specimens, which he'd come across while traveling the rough roads back from neighboring Illinois one balmy spring day.

It was a strange story, he had to admit. On the side of the road was a peculiar little man, humpbacked and bowlegged, weirdly attired in a brown tunic and peaked red cap. He looked like something out of a medieval monastery or a child's storybook. "There was a crooked man and he walked a crooked mile. / He found a crooked sixpence upon a crooked stile . . ." came to mind as Jacques watched the dwarf trying to tend to two exhausted black stallions that were dripping with sweat, foaming at the mouth, and panting with exhaustion. The little man was muttering and cursing.

"Can I be of help to you?" Jacques inquired.

The dwarf stopped his ranting and stared at Jacques. "You may, at that," he replied with a twisted grin. "How would you like to buy these noble steeds? I'll sell them to you at a price no one can match."

"Well . . ." Jacques walked over to the horses. That they were beautiful, there could be no question. They stood taller than any of his horses, and were as sleek as the finest Thoroughbreds. They obviously possessed great strength. But it seemed they had been worked practically to death.

"They're a fine pair, for sure," Jacques said. "But what the devil have they been up to? They look as if they're going to drop on the spot!"

At the word "devil," the little man jumped. "Why did you say that?" he hissed.

"What?" Jacques was bewildered. "All I meant was, these horses have been worked too hard."

"They're fine," the dwarf snapped. "With a little water and rest, they'll be up and rearing in the twinkling of an eye. Come, sir, I can tell you know horses. You'll not find the like of these anywhere else on earth."

"How much?" Jacques asked.

The dwarf quoted him a price so ridiculously low that Jacques could not suppress a whistle.

"If these horses are so valuable, why would you want to sell them so cheap?" He eyed the dwarf suspiciously.

"I've no longer any use for them," the little man replied. "I'd just as soon be free of them and on my way, and you're the only man who's passed this way today."

It was an offer Jacques couldn't refuse. He gave the little man the money, they shook hands, and he led the horses to a nearby stream. When he looked over his shoulder, the dwarf had vanished.

As the horses drank greedily, Jacques washed them down and curried them. He let them eat their fill of sweet grass and clover. Then he hitched them to his wagon and headed home.

One evening, a month or so later, there was a knock at Jacques' door. It was the strange little man.

"I've come for my horses," he announced.

"*Your* horses?" Jacques exclaimed. "What are you talking about? I bought those blacks from you, fair and square."

But even more perplexing was the fact that the unwelcome visitor had known where to find Jacques. The dwarf had never asked for his name, or inquired as to where he lived.

"How did you know where to find me?" Jacques asked.

Ignoring his question, the dwarf merely replied, "I must have the horses back. I'll return your money, with interest."

"I wouldn't sell my beauties for any amount," Jacques informed him. "You'd best be on your way."

The dwarf flew into a rage, hopping and cursing like Rumpelstiltskin. Then he left, vowing vengeance.

Although Jacques was not easily frightened, the incident unnerved him enough to hire a guard to watch the stables day and night. After several months had elapsed with no further trouble, Jacques felt safe in letting the guard go, and things return to normal.

But one night during a raging storm, he was startled by the sound of loud whinnying. Throwing on his heavy coat and hat, he went out to the stable to find his prize steeds heaving and covered with white foam, through which shone numerous bloody gashes. Jacques shook with fury. Someone not only had stolen his horses but also had whipped them unmercifully before returning them. Who else could it be but the malevolent dwarf? But why and where had he taken the steeds? And why had he returned them?

After he'd washed the horses and tended to their wounds, Jacques settled down in the barn with them, to wait and watch for any further developments. Sure enough, at the stroke of midnight he heard footsteps. Hiding behind a pile of hay, Jacques saw the barn doors open and the dwarf enter. Holding his breath, he watched as the thief led the horses out of the barn. Then he followed, in the shadows.

He couldn't believe his eyes when he saw a gleaming black coach parked outside. It was huge and ornate, and four massive black horses, just like his, were harnessed to it.

The little man harnessed Jacques' horses to the team. Determined to solve the sinister mystery, Jacques stole into the coach and hid behind the black curtains. Suddenly, he heard the resounding crack of a whip. Then, to his horror, he felt the coach lift up, up, up into the air. Looking out the window, he saw that they were flying, high above the ground, carried by the whipping, howling wind.

After what seemed like an eternity, the coach landed with a thud on the ground in a strange, pitch-black place, where it seemed no light had ever shone. Jacques was terrified. Where were they? And where were they going? It seemed as though they had left the earth and entered a no-man's-land of pure despair.

But Jacques could not lose hope. After all, his name, L'Esperance, was French for "hope." Praying the Our Father, he peered out the window and saw light. But it was not the light of deliverance. Rather, it was a hard, red glow blazing in the distance. Then, the coach was at the edge of a seething, flaming lake of molten lava that rose and bubbled as though it were a living, breathing thing. Jacques could think of only one thing: Hell's fabled Lake of Fire. He crossed himself desperately as the coach skimmed the lake and landed at the entrance of a towering black castle in the middle of the boiling, churning mass.

The coach stopped inside the courtyard, where it was, oddly enough, not blazing hot but icy cold. Shivering with the cold as much as fear, Jacques heard the rapid click of footsteps on stone. Then he heard a loud, commanding voice say, "Abbadon!"

The dwarf jumped off the coach and bowed low. "Master!"

Jacques crouched down low and peered over the edge of the coach window. He saw a tall, thin man dressed in black and the dwarf trembling on his knees.

"You got the horses?"

"For now, Master," the dwarf whispered. "But I must return them again. If their owner finds them gone, he'll surely have his farm blessed by a priest. And then you know what will happen. All heaven will break loose!"

"Stupid wretch!" screamed the master, who, Jacques reasoned, could be none other than the prince of darkness himself. "I want those horses back! Dare to fail me again, and I'll send you straight into the Lake of Fire, where you'll burn for eternity!"

With a howl, the dwarf threw himself at the Devil's feet and hugged his ankles. "Have mercy, Master," he sobbed. "I'll get them back, I promise!"

Jumping back onto the coach box, the dwarf whipped up the team, and away they flew, into the air, over the steaming lake, through the land of darkness, and back to Jacques' farm.

Jacques waited until the dwarf had unhitched his horses and led them back into the barn. Then he crept out of the coach and hid behind a large bush. When the dwarf and his evil vehicle were gone, Jacques wasted no time. He ran as fast as his feet would carry him to the local priest, rousing him from sleep, and told him the whole story.

"Father," he gasped, "Please bless my farm. Right now! There isn't even a second to waste!"

Familiar with the wiles of the evil one, the priest quickly dressed and, clutching a bottle of holy water, accompanied Jacques to his home. He blessed the farm, Jacques family, and all the animals. But when he came to the black stallions, they reared up, neighing as though they were being attacked. Jacques and his sons had all they could do to hold the horses as the priest prayed over them. The steeds screamed at the touch of holy water. Then, everyone watched in awe as the sign of the cross shone like a brand on the horses' foreheads and the great beasts sighed, as if with relief, and settled down, as docile as could be.

As the men emerged from the barn, they saw a small, twisted figure coming down the road toward the house. The dwarf was back. But as soon as he stepped across Jacques' property line, he fell backward, as if he'd smacked into an invisible wall. Cursing, he ran forward again, only to be thrown backward again.

"I'm not spending eternity in that damned lake!" he screamed. "I'll get those horses yet!"

Hell hath no fury like a goblin scorned. Hopping and dancing with rage, the dwarf uttered an incantation so vile that the priest crossed himself and covered his ears. Then, a terrible wind rose up, howling like a chorus of the damned, and spun into a tornado that whirled around the spinning, cursing dwarf. But Jacques' property remained untouched. Seeing that he was powerless before consecrated ground, the imp let loose with one final, terrible scream and disappeared, along with the tornado.

Jacques never again saw his tormentor, and the two magnificent black horses lived long and happily, as did Jacques and his family. But there's always a ready supply of holy water in Grosse Pointe. After all, when it comes to the horse-snatching devil, it's better to be safe than sorry.

Chapter 7
The Ghost of
Spring Hill Farm

I've adapted the following story, about a really nasty ghost who picked on both people and their pets, from Daniel Cohen's Dangerous Ghosts, *a fascinating collection of spooky tales. It's one of those "true" ghost stories, related to Danton Walker, a popular columnist in New York during the 1940s and 1950s, who heard it from a highly reputable source: Jeanne Owen, the president of the New York chapter of the Wine and Food Society, reputable not only because of her prestigious position but also because the incident happened to her—and forever after made her a firm believer in the unbelievable.*

In the 1940s, George Owen, a New Yorker with an avid interest in agriculture, fell in love with an old farm in California's glorious Napa Valley. Though charming, the property was not without its drawbacks. Spring Hill Farm was in an isolated spot, four miles of rough dirt road from the small town of St. Helena. Unoccupied and untended for years, the buildings were in disrepair and needed considerable remodeling. Still, Owen looked forward to the renovation and to the idyllic country life ahead.

Within six months, the dilapidated old farmhouse had been transformed into a comfortable modern home. Owen, his wife Dorothy, and their new baby moved in just in time for the beautiful Napa summer.

George's mother, Jeanne, a sophisticated New Yorker whose upscale interests included gourmet cuisine and who was president of the New York chapter of the Wine and Food Society, enjoyed getting away to visit her son and his family in quiet, unpretentious Napa—that is, until the night during one of her stays when she was awakened from her sleep by the sound of footsteps on the gravel driveway.

Jeanne looked at the clock; it was midnight. She went to the window, but even though the driveway was lit up by the full moon, she saw nothing. Yet, the footsteps continued—*crunch, crunch, crunch*, as though someone were pacing up and down the gravel path.

Mystified, she went back to bed. The footsteps continued for almost two more hours. Then, around 2:00 a.m., they stopped, and all was once again silent.

The unnerving experience was repeated every night for weeks. The family scoured the premises searching for an explanation, but came up empty-handed. They even went out to the driveway during the witching hours of midnight to two o'clock in the morning, but no one ever appeared—even though the footsteps were clearly audible.

The Owens' dog, Nick, a large German shepherd who doubled as both family pet and guard dog, always awakened as soon as the footsteps started. Growling, he would jump off the porch and race after something, or someone, that only he could see, only to return whining in pain, as if he'd been struck.

One night, as Jeanne was looking out the window onto the driveway, she saw what seemed to be the shadow of a man. "It moved to the end of the gravel drive and disappeared around the corner of the house," she recalled. "Then it disappeared along a narrow path that led to the shack on the hill."

In back of the farmhouse, up on a hill, was a broken-down, two-room shack, the purpose of which had perplexed the property's new owner, George Owen. The building was too small to live in and too large for a chicken coop. Consumed by other, more pressing repairs, George had left the shack alone and never bothered to inquire about its history.

As Jeanne stared out the window, she saw Nick jump off the porch. Barking loudly, he chased the shadow around the house and up the hill. Then, yelping with pain, he suddenly turned and ran back to the house.

When, quite shaken, Jeanne told George and Dorothy about the shadowy figure, they told her to calm down and that it was probably her imagination.

"But Nick's crying wasn't my imagination!" she insisted. "He was running after something or someone . . . exactly where I'd seen that figure disappear. And something apparently hurt him."

But there were no marks on the dog.

"He probably just got spooked by something," George reasoned.

"Yes—by a spook!" Jeanne retorted.

On several occasions, a doctor friend of the Owens would come for overnight visits. One morning at breakfast, the doctor commented, "Do any of you know who walks on the gravel drive every night in front of the house? The noise wakes me after midnight, and it's sure bothering Nick."

Now that someone outside the family had corroborated the weird occurrence, it somehow seemed more real.

Then, one evening the mystery deepened. George and Dorothy were having dinner when they saw the figure of a tall, thin, old man walk out of the back hall and toward the front door. He was scowling and smoking a cigarette. When they rushed out the door to follow him, he was gone . . . but the cigarette smell lingered.

Determined to finally learn more of the farm's history, Dorothy paid a visit to Mary Mason, an eighty-five-year-old neighbor who knew everybody's business for many years back. Oh yes, she could certainly tell Dorothy a thing or two about Spring Hill Farm.

"That old shack was once the only house on the property," Mary recalled. "Old Tom Cleary and his wife, Sarry, lived there with their three boys."

"In that tiny cabin?" Dorothy was astonished.

"Yes. It was pitiful. But Tom was a mean old coot. Kept to himself, never talked to none of us. And as tight as the devil's shoes! He'd pinch a penny 'til the Indian whooped! Poor Sarry. She was a gentle, God-fearing woman who worked as hard as the day is long and never complained about the cabin, which was worse than slaves' quarters. No electricity, no running water, nothing that would make life easier for them.

"Those boys were fine young men, though. Thank the Lord they took after their mother and not their father. They promised Sarry that someday they'd build her a 'real' house, and as soon as they were old enough, they kept that promise and built the farmhouse you're living in now. But instead of being grateful, Old Tom flew at all of them like a mad rooster and threatened to burn the new house down and them along with it.

"Well, Sarry and the boys didn't stick around to let Tom make good on that threat. They left, abandoning the house, and never came back. Tom continued to live in the shack, isolating himself more and more. People stopped looking in on him because he locked the door. Then one day, when nobody had seen him in weeks, they broke the door down and found him stone-cold dead. They buried him back of the shack, and that was the end of mean old Tom Cleary.

"But they've said for years that Spring Hill is haunted. And nobody wanted to live in it, until you folks showed up."

On that cheery note, Dorothy returned home to relay the disturbing story to George and to suggest that perhaps they ought to put the property up for sale. But George wouldn't hear of it. First of all, under the circumstances they'd probably never be able to sell it. Furthermore, he wasn't about to let some cranky old ghost run them out—not after he'd invested so much time, energy, and love into the place.

A few weeks later, Tom Cleary took his revenge—and it was Nick the dog who saved them.

Late one night when George was in San Francisco on business, Dorothy was awakened by Nick's hysterical barking. The big dog raced into her bedroom and around the bed, the barking growing more and more urgent. Then Dorothy smelled smoke. Running into the baby's room, she grabbed her child and tore downstairs. The back porch and the living room were in flames. She called the fire department and fled the house. The whole town joined forces to fight the blaze, but it was too late. The house was burned to the ground.

But even this disaster didn't light a fire under George Owen. Instead of surrendering to his malevolent adversary and moving from Spring Hill, George rebuilt the farmhouse on another site on the property. He reasoned that Tom Cleary, having destroyed the house his sons had built, as he'd vowed so long ago to do, had finally gotten his revenge and would rest in peace . . . or at least allow the Owens to live in peace.

George might have been right, because after the new house was built, they never again had any paranormal problems. Just the same, they were grateful to have Nick around to guard the premises.

"He's our hero," Dorothy said. "If it weren't for Nick, none of us would be alive. Thank heavens he's not afraid of ghosts!"

Chapter 8

The Mauthe Doog and the Demon Dogs of Anglia

On the Isle of Man in the British Isles, a malevolent ghostly dog is said to have once roamed the ancient ruins of Peel Castle, and all who encountered it supposedly met their sudden and shocking dooms. Variously known as the Mauthe Doog, the Moddey Dhoo, and the Black Dog of Death, the beast was so terrifying that it could belong to none other than the devil himself, according to legend.

The Isle of Man, located between Ireland and Great Britain in the Irish Sea, is one of the world's most beautiful and mysterious places. Some say that you can see six kingdoms from the island's highest point: Mann, Scotland, England, Ireland, Wales, and Heaven.

One of the Isle of Man's most famous landmarks is Peel Castle. The eleventh-century Viking castle is now a historic landmark open to visitors in summer. Although the walls surrounding the castle complex are amazingly intact, the buildings within its walls are mostly ruins. Centuries ago, however, it was a busy place—a soldiers' garrison as well as the occasional residence of the lord of the isle.

Castle Peel was said to be haunted by a ghostly dog—a large black spaniel with shaggy, curly hair who had two favorite spots in the castle: the guards' room and a subterranean passage connecting the guards' room with the old

Cathedral of St. Germain. The dog could often be seen curled up by the fire in the guards' room, and while the sentries grew used to its presence, none had the desire to be alone with it. There was something unfriendly, even evil, about the spaniel. If anyone so much as approached it, it would bare its teeth and growl menacingly. Nor did it have the warm, trusting brown eyes of the typical spaniel; instead, its large eyes were cold, hard, and glinting gray—like two pewter plates, as some described them.

The most famous encounter with the Mauthe Doog occurred in the seventeenth century. A group of soldiers were lounging in the guards' room, listening to the bragging of a sentry who had just gotten off duty and was in the process of getting *stocious* (in the vernacular of the Ould Sod). The ghost dog was not in the room that night, and in a burst of drunken bravado, the sentry loudly declared that he, for one, was not afraid of the Mauthe Doog. In fact, he bet his comrades that he'd go in search of the four-footed fiend and put an end to its mischief once and for all.

The other guards laughed. But off he went. For a few minutes, the other soldiers could hear his heavy footsteps reverberating on the flagstones of the passage and the clinking of his sword and armor. Then, abruptly, all was quiet, and the soldiers wondered what had happened to their friend. Suddenly, the silence was shattered by bloodcurdling screams intermingled with the most unearthly, terrifying noises. Rushing out to the corridor, the men found the foolhardy sentry lying on the stone floor, pale, shaking, his wide-open eyes transfixed with horror.

They dragged him back to the guards' room and tried to revive him with whiskey. But he could neither drink nor speak, except to babble something about the "Devil's Doog." Three days later, he died.

According to the late Irish author Elliott O'Donnell, an authority on the supernatural, "The impression the Mauthe Doog gave to all who saw it was that it was not the ghost of any material dog, but a diabolical spirit in the form of a dog."

The origins of the Mauthe Doog supposedly date back to pagan times, when black magic was practiced on the Isle of Man. Known as the Dog of Darkness, it was believed to be an omen of death for anyone who saw it.

After the sentry's death, the Mauthe Dog apparently never frequented the castle again. But in the mid-nineteenth century, a dog haunting was reported in the castle's vicinity. At night, strange animal noises could be heard coming from the grounds, motivating some of the castle's occupants to search the area for the source of the disturbance.

One night when several men were keeping watch, they reported hearing terrifying cries and howling that caused the hair on their necks to stand straight up. Suddenly, a huge, dark creature with glowing red eyes that resembled a dog "the size of a calf" rushed past them and disappeared into the woods. Then, horrible screams filled the air, followed by diabolical laughter—which, the terrified witnesses said, sounded like someone being tortured and the tormentor delighting in his victim's agony.

✛

The Mauthe Doog takes its place in a long tradition of demon dogs said to have haunted different parts of England, particularly East Anglia, for over a thousand years. The dogs are always black, usually believed to be associated with the devil, and are often thought to be an omen of death or an agent of injury. They are known as "black shuck," from the Celtic *scucca*, the Anglo-Saxon word for demon.

Descriptions of the black shuck match that of the Mauthe Doog: a shaggy creature the size of a calf, with saucer-sized eyes that sometimes glow red or green. He is a loner, attached to places instead of people, and often hangs around churchyards and cemeteries.

A famous account of the black shuck dating from 1577 describes a black demon dog that appeared in a Bungay churchyard and proceeded to wreak havoc. According to an old pamphlet, by the time the unearthly black beast departed, two parishioners were dead at their prayers and another was "as shrunken as a piece of leather burned in a hot fire." The dreadful incident was corroborated by the Reverend Abraham Fleming in his 1577 account titled "A Straunge and Terrible Wunder. . . ."

> This black dog, or the divel in such a likenesse (God hee knoweth al who worketh all) runing all along down the body of the church with great swiftnesse, and incredible haste, among the people, in a visible fourm and shape, passed between two persons, as they were kneeling uppon their knees, and occupied in prayer as it seemed, wrung the necks of them bothe at one instant clene backward, in somuch that even at the mome[n]t where they kneeled, they stra[n]gely dyed.

In general, however, the black shuck is believed to be harmless unless crossed. Then, like the Mauthe Doog, it will attack, leaving its victim senseless. Death usually follows within a few days.

Stories of the black shuck vary from region to region. The black shuck of Clopton Hall in Stowmarket in Suffolk, England, is said to stand guard over a gold stash, deterring would-be thieves with his monklike body and houndlike head.

In Norfolk, the site of many a werewolf legend, the shuck resembles a black wolf and shrieks louder than the wind on a stormy night. Numerous people have reported sensing the monster padding behind them and feeling its icy breath on their necks as they walked at night, and motorists have reported swerving to avoid the phantom animal as it crossed the road.

The Yorkshire shuck, a monstrous dog with huge fangs and claws, appears only after dark. Both the Yorkshire and Norfolk legends maintain that no one can set eyes upon the black shuck and live, while in Cambridgeshire, the black shuck's appearance is believed to warn of a death in the family.

Wherever the black shuck of the British Isles roams, it is never safe to travel alone . . . unless you're accompanied by a companion who is a descendant of Ean MacEndroe of Loch Ewe. Ean once rescued a fairy, and in return he and his descendants were granted perpetual immunity from the power of the black dogs.

Demon dogs are not confined to the British Isles. The next chapter tells the story of the five devil dogs of Cedar Cliff, North Carolina, who came out of nowhere to avenge the murder of some Yankee marauders one night in 1865.

Chapter 9

The Devil Dogs of Cedar Cliff

If the mountains of North Carolina could talk, they'd tell many a ghost story. And one of the most sinister is the tale of the devil dogs— huge, threatening canines reputed to haunt Cedar Cliff, a remote and rocky mountain community overlooking the Tuckasegee River. This story, adapted form Randy Russell and Janet Barnett's Ghost Dogs of the South, *is an actual account of an elderly woman who was one of the few souls brave enough to have lived near Cedar Cliff and unfortunate enough to have had a personal encounter with the "dogs of hell" at the end of the Civil War.*

Annie O'Rourke was a true mountain woman, from the deep creases in her weather-beaten face to the worn hem of her handmade calico skirt. She lived all her life in a rustic cabin near Cedar Cliff in North Carolina, and she was a walking compendium of all the region's ballads, legends, and ghost stories, some of which were true and some of which weren't. Annie herself was the central character in one of Cedar Cliff's true ghost stories, which she related to a folklore professor in 1931, when she was seventy-eight years old. At least she insisted it was true. And what reason would an old woman soon to meet her maker have to lie?

In 1865, Annie was twelve years old, and the Civil War had just ended, though its hot breath could still be felt on the neck of the shamed, defeated South. Most of the mountain men in the region had gone off to fight in the war and never returned, leaving their womenfolk to shoulder the tough task of living. The women, of course, were used to hard work and deprivation, and they faced their fate with characteristic fortitude. They managed to keep their children fed and clothed, the Lord only knew how. But their strength and courage were sorely tested when Yankee troops moved into the mountains to establish rule over the suffering inhabitants.

"They wore their uniforms and carried their guns and told us what to do," Annie recalled, her voice still seething with bitterness. "They made us feed them and their horses, too. They ransacked our property—took our livestock and moved right into our homes, forcing us to live in our barns."

Three Yankees in particular made life hell for Annie and her family. They set up camp on Cedar Cliff and were meaner than the others. They picked on the war widows, one of whom was Annie's mother, visiting from camp whenever they felt like it and forcing themselves on the women and girls.

Annie lived in fear of what the men might do. When one of the Yankees made her dance with him, walking her around the room to invisible music, and tried to make her kiss him, she fought back. He retreated, but Annie's mother wasn't about to sit by any longer. She knew she had to take matters into her own hands and quickly. She gathered two other widows whom the Yankee trio had singled out, and together they devised a plan.

The Yankees thought they were sitting pretty, the masters of helpless females. They were completely unaware that these tough mountain women had guns and knew how to use them. They'd had to take over for the absent menfolk, after all, and so they'd learned to chop wood and hunt.

Annie's mother often went out, gun in hand, to bring back dinner—squirrel, rabbit, the occasional deer; she was a good shot, and her family never starved.

When the Yankees came, the women had hidden the guns they used for hunting and protection as well as the knives they used for skinning, gutting, and cooking. After their meeting, the women got their guns out and sneaked on to Cedar Cliff, accompanied by twelve-year-old Annie and the sixteen-year-old daughter of one of the women.

Although hiking up the mountain toting the heavy guns was an arduous task, their mission gave them strength. Soon, they spotted the Yankees' horses tied to trees. They held their breath, praying that the animals wouldn't give them away, but the horses merely watched them with mild interest.

The three Yankees lay on blankets outside the tent they had pitched on Cedar Cliff, fast asleep and snoring. The three women wasted no time. Creeping over to their quarry, they put their guns to the sleeping men's heads and fired all at the same time, killing the Yankees instantly.

Annie felt a twinge of remorse at the taking of human life, however odious. But her mother—who might well have coined the phrase *The only good Yankee is a dead Yankee*—was proud that, thanks to her and the other two women, three fewer Yankees were taking up space on God's earth.

Now that their mission was accomplished, though, what were they to do with the bodies? They talked it over. Leaving the corpses there was too dangerous, the risk of getting caught and hanged too high. Nor did they see fit to live as fugitives, hiding out the rest of their days over in Tennessee, God forbid.

"We were homefolks," Annie observed. "We weren't renegades."

So the women returned home to hide the murder weapons and get their shovels. Then, they trudged back to Cedar Cliff. They didn't bring a wagon; it would be impossible to get one up the steep, rocky mountain. When they reached the camp, they untied the Yankees' horses and ran them off. Then they set about digging their victims' graves—hard labor, indeed. They exhausted themselves trying to get through the rock to the hard, dry ground. It took all morning to dig a hole deep enough for all three men. After they'd thrown in the bodies, the women carried piles of rocks and strewed them around over the burial pit. Nobody would ever have suspected it was a grave.

Now, one of the widows had done something that, to Annie's mother, boded ill. Before they'd buried the men, she'd started screaming and cursing. Then she made for the Yankee she'd killed and sliced his body to shreds. Annie's mother tried to stop her. Such postmortem violence was a real sin, one that could bring harm to all of them. When it came to desecrating the dead, God had his ways of teaching people a lesson.

When they reached the bottom of the mountain, the woman with the knife suddenly gave a shout. Coming toward them were five huge, black dogs—one for each of them. But these weren't regular dogs. They were massive and sleek, like panthers, with big, red mouths. Oddly enough, they didn't bark; the only sound coming from them was their heavy breathing.

"The devil dogs!" Annie's mother whispered.

Annie stood stock-still in terror. Many were the tales of the devil dogs that she'd heard from her father and grandfather, which made for spine-chilling listening by the fire on the clear, cool autumn nights when the moon hid behind dark clouds and the dead leaves tossed in the restless wind. The beasts were really demons disguised as dogs. If you saw one, you were to instantly avert your eyes, utter the name of Jesus, and run like the devil himself was after you—because he was. The dog's appearance always portended someone's death, and if you met its fiery eyes, that death could be yours.

The dogs had followed the women down from Cedar Cliff. It was clear, said Annie, that they could never return to the place. The devil dogs wouldn't let them.

"Those dogs came up from hell when we buried those Yankees," Annie maintained. "They guarded Cedar Cliff from then on, and they weren't leaving until the last of us was dead."

Sure enough, as the women died, one by one, the dogs disappeared, until, sixty-five years later, only one remained.

"He's the devil," Annie shrugged. "He's waiting on me, don't you know. When I die, that dog on Cedar Cliff will be gone. But at least one thing's for sure: If I go to heaven, he won't be going with me!"

Chapter 10

Julie

The following is a cautionary tale for bargain hunters. When a London family looking for a house to rent came upon a residence in the upscale Maida Vale district with an amazingly low price tag, they immediately jumped on it. No one happened to mention that the house was haunted. But their cat, Julie, didn't need to be told. She discovered it all on her own.

In the 1920s, a family by the name of Foxworthy signed a three-year lease on a stately old home in London's fashionable Maida Vale district. Everyone—Maurice Foxworthy, his wife, Dorothy, and their eighteen-year-old daughter, Margaret—was delighted with the new digs. Everyone, that is, except for their cat, Julie.

Julie was an affectionate tabby who generally had no trouble acclimating to her surroundings. But no sooner was she brought into the parlor of the new house and let out of her carrier than she began acting restless and wary.

As cats will, Julie immediately went exploring. Her travels led her down into the basement, where she suddenly let out a wild scream. Running downstairs, Margaret discovered Julie in a state—up on her tiptoes, tail high, fur sticking out as though she'd suddenly been plugged into an electrical socket, staring ahead and hissing loudly at an empty room.

"Julie! Julie!" Margaret called to her.

The cat always came when she heard Margaret's voice, but this time she ignored her mistress and remained rooted to the spot, hissing and spitting.

Margaret searched the basement, trying to discover the source of Julie's agitation. When she went into the room that the cat was fixated on, she felt a chill. *No doubt, the dampness,* she thought. But she also felt uncomfortable, as though somehow she wasn't welcome in that room. Yet, no one was there, and Margaret could find nothing unusual about the room. Furnished simply, it might at one time have been a maid's or servant's quarters. It smelled slightly musty, as though it had not been occupied for a long time.

"Come, Julie! Come, little girl," she called to the cat, gesturing for it to join her.

Julie stood still, hesitating, and then ventured slowly toward Margaret. But she stopped at the threshold and let out a low growl. Then she suddenly jumped backward with another loud scream and bolted upstairs.

The family was mystified by Julie's behavior. But they also knew that animals can sense things humans can't and that cats, in particular, have a reputation for being psychic.

A week or two went by. Julie settled into the new house, although she refused to go near the basement again. It was almost Christmas, and the house looked so festive and welcoming that the disturbing incident in the basement was forgotten.

One afternoon, Margaret came home from shopping and entered the house by way of the basement to take off her wet boots. Suddenly, she felt someone watching her. She turned to see an old woman looking at her from the doorway of the room that had so upset Julie. Margaret was taken aback, not only by the stranger's presence but also by her attire. She was dressed in an old-fashioned black gown with a white handkerchief pinned across her bosom. On her head was a close-fitting white cap, the kind servants wore a couple of centuries before. Had her parents engaged a new maid or housekeeper?

"Hello, whoever you are," Margaret nodded in greeting. "Would you mind taking these boots and putting them by the fire to dry out?"

Carelessly, Margaret tossed the high-heeled boots in her direction. But to her astonishment, the boots went right through the old woman! Then, as Margaret watched in horror, the apparition turned around and disappeared through the stone wall.

When she could collect herself, Margaret raced upstairs and almost collided with her mother in the hall.

"Why, Maggie, what's wrong?" Mrs. Foxworthy asked her breathless and shaken daughter.

"I saw a ghost!" Margaret cried. "An old woman, down in the basement. . . ." She stopped short and pointed to the staircase leading to the upper floors. "That's her! That's the woman!" she exclaimed.

Mrs. Foxworthy looked toward the stairs. She, too, saw the figure Margaret described, going slowly up toward the second floor, moving absolutely silently.

"Stop!" she cried. "Who are you?"

As if deaf, the woman kept going. Mrs. Foxworthy quickly ran up the stairs, followed by Margaret. But when she was halfway up the second flight, she saw the figure vanish, literally into thin air.

"Well!" said Mrs. Foxworthy. "It looks like we've got a ghost!"

It wasn't all that unusual. After all, in England "hants" go with houses like biscuits go with tea. As long as the ghost seemed harmless, Mrs. Foxworthy was actually pleased. It was something to talk about.

But to Mrs. Foxworthy's disappointment, the apparition did not reappear, and all was back to boring old normal—until a couple of weeks later, when Mr. Foxworthy, who liked to stay up late, was reading in his study and heard a loud rapping. Going into the hall, he quietly ascended the stairs, where he found the cause of the noise: ivy tapping against the glass of the open window on the landing overlooking the garden.

Breathing a sigh of relief, Mr. Foxworthy was about to return to his study when the tapping grew louder. Then a draft of cold air rushed past him, and the front door began to rattle as though it were about to come off its hinges. It sounded for all the world like someone, or something, was working the door handle in a concerted effort to get into the house.

Then, Mr. Foxworthy felt something bump into him, the very clear sensation of having collided with an object, but nothing there. He made another attempt to descend the stairs but again ran into an invisible blockage. His fear mounting, he tried going up the stairs, whereupon he felt, as he later told his wife and daughter, something "cold and clammy" grab him by the throat and start to choke him. The poor man tried to extricate himself from the stranglehold, but there was nothing to grab onto. Whatever was attacking him was completely invisible and intangible. Gasping and sputtering, he tried in vain to cry out for help but managed to utter merely a small croak. Just as he began to lose consciousness, he heard Margaret's voice.

"Father! Father! Whatever is the matter?"

At that instant, the "thing" released its hold, and Mr. Foxworthy felt the air rushing back into his lungs, accompanied by a great sense of relief as his ghostly assailant vanished. Margaret came upon him standing shakily on the stairs, clutching the banister and looking ghastly pale.

By this time, Mrs. Foxworthy had come out to see what was going on. When her husband stammered out the story, she was no longer pleased about having a pet ghost.

"Something evil is here," she declared. "We should either get a priest to exorcise the house or pack up and get out."

Mr. Foxworthy told his wife to calm down. He would look into the matter, he assured her.

Meanwhile, Julie had begun acting up again. Having abandoned the basement for the upstairs, she was fond of wandering around the upper stories of the house during the daytime but refused to go to that area of the house after dark. As soon as the sun began to set, the cat would race downstairs and into the parlor or kitchen, where she would curl up in a comfortable spot and remain until morning.

After Mr. Foxworthy's unnerving experience with the ghostly strangler, Julie began acting panicky even when she was downstairs. She would whine and pace, and if anyone closed the door to the room she happened to be in, the little cat would claw at it frantically, trying to get out.

Spring came and along with it a visit from the Foxworthy's eldest daughter, Petulia—"Pet"—and her only child, Beth. The little girl loved animals and instantly made friends with Julie.

One evening, Beth was playing in the breakfast room when Pet heard a commotion coming from that quarter. Running to check on her daughter, she found Beth shaking her head in exasperation.

"What was all that noise I heard?" Pet asked.

"It was Julie," Beth replied. "She had some sort of fit! I couldn't believe how jealous she got. I was playing with her when another little animal came into the room and tried to join in."

"Another animal?" Pet was mystified. "What sort of animal?"

"I'm not exactly sure, Mummy," Beth said. "I couldn't make it out. It was rather misty looking, with long, furry ears, and it scuttled about so fast I couldn't catch it. Julie got very nasty and hissed and spat at the poor little thing. I told her to behave, but she just ran to the door and started scratching at it and meowing, so I let her out. Look at the marks she made! Granny will be mad, won't she?"

"What happened to the strange animal?" Pet asked.

"Oh, I trapped it!" Beth laughed. She led her mother to a small cupboard next to the fireplace. "It ran in there, and I shut the door and bolted it."

"I don't hear anything," said her mother.

"It must be there still," Beth insisted. "It couldn't have gotten out."

The child drew back the bolt and threw the door open. But the cupboard was empty.

From then on, Julie refused to go into the breakfast room. It seemed her available operating space was decreasing by the day.

One would think that, by then, the Foxworthys would have gotten the hint and departed the creepy premises posthaste. But it apparently took more than a ghostly old woman, a murderous specter, and an unidentified four-footed apparition to convince them that their home was not conducive to their health.

The night after Beth and Julie saw the ghost creature, Pet was awakened in the middle of the night by the strong sensation of a presence by the bed. Maggie lay beside her, fast asleep, and Beth was sleeping peacefully in a small bed beside them. Pet looked around and saw nothing. Nonetheless, the eerie feeling that someone else was in the room grew increasingly more pronounced. Pet could not talk herself out of the fear that was building inside of her.

Then, on the wall facing her Pet saw the sinister shadow of a hand. She waved her own hands and then the pillow and various other objects to see whether she could make the shadow disappear. But it remained, fingers outstretched, as if reaching for something. It looked like the hand of an old woman, with bony knuckles. In an extra ghoulish twist, the top of the little finger was missing.

Pet felt a sense of revulsion so overwhelming that for a moment she thought she was going to be sick. Then, to her complete horror, the shadowy hand began to creep up the wall and over the ceiling, scuttling like a huge spider until it was hovering over her head. Suddenly, it vanished, and the next thing Pet knew, Maggie was writhing and crying out in her sleep, her eyes still closed but her face convulsed in pain. She seemed to be having a nightmare. Pet grabbed her sister and shook her violently. Margaret awoke, gasping for breath.

"Thank heavens you woke me!" she cried. "I was having the most horrible dream. Someone was trying to strangle me! But it felt so real, like it was actually happening. I can still feel those awful bony fingers, squeezing my windpipe!"

When Pet told her sister about the shadowy hand, Maggie screamed, waking Beth. Pet rushed to her daughter, grabbed her, and took her into her own bed.

"We're going home first thing in the morning," she declared.

Both Pet and Maggie remained awake the rest of the night, candles burning all around them.

Well, this last chilling incident finally prompted Mr. Foxworthy to do some investigating. He discovered that the house had long had the reputation of being haunted, and he had little trouble convincing the landlord to terminate his lease. The Foxworthys found another house to rent and quickly moved out of the Maida Vale house of terror. As for Julie, she was more than happy to leave the ghosts behind and return to normal cat life.

Chapter 11

The Mystery House Tragedy

It's bad enough when ghosts go bad and attack people. But when they go after innocent animals, it's time for eternal life without parole at the Ghost Big House. At the lovely but deadly London villa in this story, neither man nor beast was safe from the wrath of a vengeful ghost that none could say for sure was man or beast.

Just before the First World War, a small villa near the Crystal Palace in London, England, was dubbed "the mystery house" by locals. The owners did not live there, and it always seemed to be for rent, as whoever moved in moved out almost as quickly.

The mystery house had stood empty for over a year when a family named Trent moved in.

In those days, it was the custom among the upper classes in England for husbands and wives to have separate bedrooms. One night shortly after the family had settled into their new digs, Mrs. Trent was awakened by the frantic whining of her black poodle, Cherry, and the violent goings on in her bed— with pillows moving about and the bedstead shaking as if in an earthquake. As Mrs. Trent jumped out of the bed, she thought she saw the covers moving as well. Her first thought was that an animal had somehow gotten into the bed. But there was nothing under the sheets and pillows.

Cautiously, Mrs. Trent crawled back into bed and waited. But whatever had been responsible for the ruckus seemed to have departed. Cherry jumped into bed with her, and the two of them fell back asleep.

At breakfast, Mrs. Trent mentioned the weird incident to her husband.

"I thought I heard Cherry whining," he remarked.

"Well, why didn't you come in to see what was the matter?" Mrs. Trent demanded.

Mr. Trent shrugged. "By the time I was awake enough to get up, she'd stopped." He then suggested, with manly skepticism, that his wife might have been having a very realistic dream.

"I did not dream it!" Mrs. Trent insisted. "I saw the pillows moving, and that bed was shaking as sure as I'm sitting here! And what of Cherry? Was she dreaming as well?"

That night, Cherry jumped up on Mr. Trent's bed, frantically trying to get his attention. The little dog whined and whined, and when Mr. Trent sleepily turned away from her, she began to bark so insistently that he sat up at last.

"For the love of God, what is it?" he mumbled.

Cherry jumped off the bed and raced out of the room, looking over her shoulder to make sure Mr. Trent was following her. Just then, a bloodcurdling scream came from his wife's room. Leaping out of bed, Mr. Trent rushed in to find her trying to push a pillow away from her face, fighting an invisible adversary who seemed to be hell-bent—literally—on suffocating her.

Cherry was hysterical, growling, baring her teeth, barking wildly at someone that only she seemed to be able to see. Mr. Trent grabbed the pillow, but he, too, struggled fiercely with the entity. Finally, he felt the force dissipate, and the pillow fell to the floor.

Mrs. Trent was so exhausted and unnerved that it took several hours before she could recount what exactly had happened. All she remembered was waking up from a terrible dream and finding her pillow over her face. She was sure someone was trying to smother her.

Mr. Trent suggested that his wife trade rooms with him. She did, and there were no further incidents . . . until she, the children, and the maid took off for an afternoon out, leaving Mr. Trent alone in the house. It wasn't long before he heard loud, loping footfalls behind him. As he ascended the stairs, the footfalls followed, becoming increasingly louder and closer, as if something were trying to overtake him. Turning around, he yelled, "Damn it! Show yourself, whoever or whatever you are!"

Suddenly, all fell silent—too silent. The footfalls stopped, and the house became deathly still.

The Trents had had enough. They left the villa in haste.

A week later, it was let to a Miss Cattling, formerly of the theater. She arrived with an entourage of little dogs— three dachshunds and four Pomeranians.

Although Miss Cattling was quite comfortable in her new quarters, her dogs were not. They whined and growled, particularly at night, huddling together in fear. Miss Cattling found their behavior odd but not inexplicable; they probably were just adjusting to the strange new surroundings, she reasoned.

Then, one evening about a week after her arrival, Miss Cattling heard one of the Poms yelping as if it were hurt. She hastened to her bedroom, where she saw the tiny dog lying on the floor, unconscious. Upon examining it, Miss Cattling found, to her horror, that it was dead. She had hardly begun to deal with the shock when she noticed something fantastic out of the corner of her eye: One of the pillows on her bed was standing on end. As she approached it, things turned even more bizarre. The pillow assumed the shape of a hideous face—whether human or animal, she couldn't say. It had a huge, long nose, giant fangs, and two deep-set, gleaming black eyes, and seemed to be grinning maniacally.

Enraged, Miss Cattling grabbed the pillow and flung it to the floor. "You killed my dog, you monster!" she screamed. "But you won't get me! You won't!"

Now you'd think that after a horrible experience like this, Miss Cattling would have packed up her dogs and headed for the hills. But for reasons unknown, she continued to live at the villa.

For a while, things were calm. Then, upon returning from walking the dogs one night, she found the house in pitch darkness. While she was in the hall groping around for matches with which to light the gas lantern, someone or something slipped a box of them into her hand. Petrified, she stood there, listening for a sound. But there was none. Then, striking a match, she peered around. There was no one. Who had slipped her the matches? And why?

The next morning, as she was dressing, the dogs began to whimper. Then they shot under the bed, where they huddled together, refusing to come out. Presently, Miss Cattling heard a long sigh close to her elbow. Again, no one was in the room—no one visible to *her*, anyway. She wished the dogs could tell her what they were seeing.

That evening, Miss Cattling entertained friends. They were playing cards when one of the guests exclaimed, "Look at that picture!"

Everyone glanced over at the wall, where an old gilt-framed engraving was swaying violently. If the movement had been caused by the wind coming in through the open window, the other pictures would have also been affected, but they remained motionless. Besides, the night was very calm and still.

"It would take a great gust of wind to make that picture dance around like that," Miss Cattling observed.

Then, just as suddenly as the picture had begun to move, it became still. In fact, a strange silence descended on the entire room.

Miss Cattling left soon afterward, and the villa remained vacant for at least a year.

One of the villa's last occupants was a Mrs. Eveley, who rented the house for six months with her grown daughter, Barbara, and two servants. The ghosts wasted no time with the new tenants. On the very first night of their arrival, Barbara awoke in the middle of the night to find the tall figure of a man in black standing over her bed. He was quite visible in the moonlight that flooded the room. Petrified, she cried out. This seemed to irritate the man, who rudely snatched the bedclothes off of her and began to shake the bed vigorously up and down. When he'd finished making his statement, the intruder backed off and faded away before her terrified eyes.

When she recovered from the shock, Barbara ran into her mother's room and told her what had happened. A no-nonsense woman, Mrs. Eveley was convinced there was a logical, if unpleasant, explanation: It was a burglar, pure and simple. And she wasn't about to let him get away.

"But, Mother!" Barbara protested. "I saw him disappear right in front of me! He just faded away!"

"Pish, tush, and pshaw!" Mrs. Eveley snorted.

She ordered the servants to search the house with her. They looked in every room, but found no one. Nor, as far as they could ascertain, had anything been taken.

A week or two later, the entire household was awakened in the early morning hours by the sound of hammering. It seemed to be coming up from the basement. The servants refused to check it out, so Mrs. Eveley grabbed a candle and went down by herself to investigate. What she found unnerved even her: In the middle of the floor stood a large black coffin. Mrs. Eveley was so horrified that she didn't even venture to see if it was empty or occupied. She fainted on the spot.

Needless to say, Mrs. Eveley and her household did not hang around the mystery house after that. They fled as soon as they could pack up their things.

Who, or what, was haunting the mystery house? All anyone knew was that the original owner was a man of decidedly bad reputation. Perhaps, as many believed, the hauntings were caused by his evil earthbound spirit. Or perhaps some terrible event had occurred in the house or on the site before the house was built. Until dogs can talk, we'll never know.

Chapter 12
Haunted Zoos

With their notorious reputations for inflicting anguish and misery on innocent beasts, zoos have traditionally been natural breeding grounds for animal hauntings. Although today's zoos are far more humane and accommodating to the needs of their wild captives, the zoos of the past were basically prisons and torture chambers, and the ghosts of many of their victims continue to prowl their paths, unable to liberate themselves from their earthly chains.

Famed pet psychic Laura Stinchfield is no stranger to paranormal pet cases. The internationally known animal trainer and "animal communicator" grew up on a horse farm in Westchester County, New York, and from an early age had an extraordinary connection to animals.

"As far back as I can remember, I knew what animals were thinking and feeling," Laura said. "I had no idea that not everyone understood them to the degree that I did."

For sensitives like Laura, zoos are painful territory. Today, such attractions are admittedly more hospitable to their residents, but the old zoos were essentially places of horror for the frightened, helpless animal captives who spent their unhappy lives confined in cruelly small spaces and were often abused and starved, while onlookers paid to gawk at their misery. The old Griffith Park Zoo in Los Angeles is a dismal reminder of the zoos of the past, and in 2010, Laura and a TV crew visited the site where it once existed. The resulting experience was one the pet psychic would never want to repeat.

"The old Griffith Park Zoo was in operation from 1912 to 1965, before it moved two miles down the road to its current location," she noted on her blog. "It had been suggested to me that I go to the ruins of this zoo to see what I might sense."

A crew that included Laura's assistant/producer, four camera people, and two dogs—Laura's Aussie, Storm King, and her assistant's dog, Ventura—embarked on the adventure with enthusiasm. But as soon as Laura approached the ruins, enthusiasm turned to revulsion. The psychic buckled over with nausea as she entered what remained of the cages.

"The large animal enclosures are small, dark, and gloomy. Some of the cages are open, and we are able to walk through long, dark, steep passageways to what must have been the nighttime holding pens. Satanic designs are painted on the walls, and litter crowds the corners.

"In my mind's eye, cats like lions, tigers, servals, bobcats, cougars, and leopards are weaving past me. They are skeletons with skin, sick to their stomachs, and fearful of coming out into the light. In a dark hallway, I see an image of a small spotted cat."

The ghosts were speaking to Laura, saying, "We are sick. We don't want to have to walk by the dead one, but every night they make us. Our eyes are stinging, and our stomachs hurt. Two of the bigger cats have tried to kill each other for food. We all used to be in the wild. They captured us and brought us here. Why? People won't leave us alone. They come here and stare at us. We are scared to move on to the bright light. It's too bright for us."

Laura's dog Storm was equally affected. He telepathically communicated what he was hearing. "They are saying that people electrocuted them with poles. Why would people do that? Mom, they have metal collars on them that are too tight. Why don't their moms take them off?"

The rest of the crew reported feeling "cramped and suffocating."

Laura went to work. "Outside in a larger enclosure, I sit and call in animals that have already passed over to come and take the animals that have been left behind. I contemplate why a higher power has not already come for them. It seems so cruel. I explain to the cats that they must go toward the light even though their eyes burn. I tell them they will feel safe and free once again. I bow my head. I pray. I ask for a sign that I have been heard. I raise my head and see my initials written in white on two of the walls next to me. I think about coincidences, and I long for a more convincing sign."

The horror continued to unfold. "There is more suffering I sense: a monkey accidentally hanging himself from spinning from psychosis; elephants with sore, infected feet; and a komodo dragon peering out of the darkness," Laura wrote. "Even the skeptics bow their heads. The suffering seems to stick to our breaths."

Later, Laura's assistant producer researched the zoo and discovered that during World War II, when beef was on the ration list, the zoo was forced to feed the cats horsemeat, with disastrous results. All of the cats at the zoo sickened and died.

"My communications are validated, but I am not thrilled," Laura says. "I think of the spirits that are still trapped within their enclosures, and I pray that their souls are released."

✛

The Cincinnati Zoo, the second oldest zoo in America, is another famous animal-haunting ground. Built in 1875, its reptile house is classified as the oldest zoo building in the Western Hemisphere. Within its aged walls, the ghosts still wander the premises in an endless quest for freedom.

It is said that a lion or lioness haunts the zoo. Visitors have repeatedly seen it walking the paths and watching the passersby. Witnesses state that the huge cat has appeared when they have been walking down a remote path. When they turn to run, the sounds of animal footfalls follow them, increasing in speed the faster they try to get away. But when they're sure the lion is about to pounce and they turn around, there is nothing behind them.

Others have reported seeing glowing green lion eyes peering out at them from the brush down a certain dark, out-of-the-way path and then walking slowly in the other direction, hoping the lion won't follow them. When they turned to look back, there was no evidence of any beast anywhere.

⁂

Across the sea at the famously haunted Isle of Wight Zoo, both animal and human ghosts have been regularly sighted. The zoo dates from the mid-nineteenth century and was formerly built as Sandown Fort. The keepers have reported seeing the ghost of a young soldier who was cut in half in a tragic accident in 1888, and they say "something" tampers with the electric lights in the old tunnels and near the spot where the soldier was split in two when an eighteen-ton gun rolled backward.

A ghostly elephant has been heard, its trumpeting cries echoing faintly near the place where the elephant cages once were. Even in broad daylight, visitors claim to have seen the transparent shapes of zebras, cougars, and other wildlife soundlessly floating in and out of the bushes.

✛

Laura Stinchfield encourages all of us to keep the zoo ghosts in our prayers and to try to psychically guide them out of their earthbound prisons and into the light.

"Please envision them being brave and venturing toward the light," she advises. "Imagine the cage doors open and the angels of their species coming to guide them. Imagine that the love we have for the ones that suffer sets them free."

Chapter 13

The Wolf Girl

While the werewolves of folklore and literature are always male, women, too, have bonded with wolves and received their mixed blessing. One such she-wolf was Emily Burt, a young girl born on a Georgia plantation in 1841, whose life changed forever when she came upon a motherless lupine baby in the hollow of an ancient tree.

The mystique of the wolf is an ancient and powerful one. While wolves are wily and dangerous beasts, they also are faithful to their mates and devoted to their families. Although wolves kill innocent creatures, they do so with speed, grace, and enviable precision. In some cultures, the wolf is thought to possess powers both magical and demonic.

The myth (or is it a myth?) of the werewolf is that of wolf power over man and wolf union with man. According to legend, a human that has been bitten by a wolf turns into a werewolf when the moon is full each month, doing horrible wolf deeds by night and awakening in human form at dawn, consumed with terror over his nocturnal crimes, the horror of which he can only guess.

Yet, as ghastly as the werewolf's fate is, it is also a strange blessing, for those possessed by the wolf are also given its gifts: the gift of senses so sharp that one can hear, see, and smell for miles; the gift of physical prowess so swift and elegant that the recipient nearly flies with the birds; the gift of energy so primal and intense that it seems one has never known life until now. Keen of sense and fleet of foot, the wolf man—or wolf woman—becomes one with the most mystical aspects of nature and privy to the inner workings of the universe.

⁜

The fascinating book *Ghost Dogs of the South,* written by Randy Russell and Janet Barnett, contains an unusual story that has become part of the local folklore of Talbot County, Georgia. The following is adapted from that account.

Emily Burt was a fortunate child. Born into a well-to-do family, she spent her early years in carefree luxury on the family's plantation in Georgia. Her twelfth birthday was a particularly happy occasion; on that day, her parents gave her a stunning silver locket engraved with her initials and with a finely crafted flower that seemed to blaze like a diamond in the center of the piece. Emily was so taken with the beautiful present that she longed to wear it every minute. But her parents informed her firmly that she was never to wear it out of the house and that it was to be kept in her room whenever she took it off.

The rules were bent, however, at Emily's twelfth birthday party, when she was allowed to show off the locket at a supper on the lawn. One of the guests at the party was a fourteen-year-old boy named Owen, who was as smitten with Emily as she was with her locket. He tried to get her attention by turning cartwheels, but when he fell in a clumsy heap, Emily only laughed at him. Determined to win her interest, he approached her shyly at last.

"I have something for you," he said.

"A birthday present?" she asked.

"Sort of."

"Is it as pretty as this?" Emily proudly touched her precious locket. "My parents gave it to me. It's the loveliest birthday gift I've ever gotten."

"Well, no," Owen stammered. "It's not like that. Not fancy or shiny, or meant to be showed off."

"What is it then?" demanded Emily.

"I can't tell you. You've got to come with me, so I can show you."

"Where is it?"

"In the woods."

Despite her spotless new white dress and the fact that she had no business leaving her own party, Emily followed the lanky, towheaded boy eagerly. At first she wasn't afraid; the woods surrounding the estate had been her playground ever since she could remember. But as they went deeper and deeper into them, she grew uneasy.

"How much farther, Owen?" she called to her guide, who was far ahead of her. "I'm not supposed to be out here, you know. Mama and Papa will worry, and then they'll get madder than the cat that missed the fish fry."

"Over here," Owen called. He was standing by a majestic old oak tree. "Look."

He gestured to a hollow in the tree. Emily stuck her head inside and found herself looking into the frightened eyes of a tiny puppy nestled on a bed of leaves.

"A puppy!" she exclaimed. "For me?"

"He's not a puppy," said Owen.

"What is he then?" Emily snorted. "A parrot?"

"He's a wolf."

"He is not!" Emily argued. "He's a puppy—the cutest, sweetest puppy in the world. And you put him there for me. Oh, Owen, you're sweet."

Owen blushed. But being honest, he shook his head.

"I didn't put him there. His mother did. She hid him, 'cause they were after her for killing sheep. They got her the other day, down by the creek."

"Then he's an orphan." Emily reached inside the tree and stroked the tiny, fuzzy head. "I'm taking him home. He must be so hungry."

"You can't do that," Owen cautioned. "They'll kill him when they find him. They've killed all the wolves around here."

"Then you're never to say a word about him." Emily gathered up the baby wolf in her arms. "Promise?"

"How are you going to keep him without anybody finding out?"

"I'll hide him in the barn." Emily nuzzled the furry bundle. "Besides, I still think he's a puppy. When he starts to grow, he'll turn into a dog, and Mama and Papa will let me keep him, I know."

Emily carried the pup home and found a wooden box for him in the horse barn. She made a bed of straw for the little thing and brought it some milk. After lapping it all up hungrily, the wolf pup promptly fell asleep. Emily hid the box in a corner in the back of the barn and covered it with a flour sack. Then she returned, somewhat disheveled, to the party she had left more than an hour before.

"Where were you, young lady?" Her father demanded. "You just disappeared! And look at you! How did you get so filthy, in your new dress, no less?"

"I'm sorry, Papa," Emily stammered, looking down at her once pristine dress, now soiled with dirt and puppy hair. "I was playing with Owen Talbot."

"You're twelve years old now, Emily," her mother said firmly. "You're a young woman, not a tomboy like you used to be. Those days are over. Go inside and clean yourself up, and start acting your age."

Grateful not to have to do any more explaining, Emily nodded and ran inside the house. She washed up, combed her hair, and changed into a clean frock. Then, unable to resist checking in on the puppy, she ran back to the barn.

The puppy was still asleep. He looked so adorable, so innocent. She knelt down and lifted him out of his box, cuddling him against her. He opened his sleepy little eyes and licked her. Then he nibbled at her finger. But unlike a normal newborn puppy, this little fellow had teeth—razor sharp teeth that bit into her flesh and drew blood. Emily cried out and pulled her finger away. As she looked at the bright red drop of blood on her fingertip, Emily realized what she had to do. She pulled some hairs from the puppy's soft tail and placed them on her finger. It was an Old South remedy for dog bite, said to prevent rabies and protect against evil spirits.

Then she had a strange idea. She wasn't sure what possessed her, but she found some small scissors and cut more hair from the puppy's back. That night, before climbing into bed, she took out her silver locket and put the strand of puppy hair inside it. Then she fell asleep.

As the moon rose high in the sky and Emily slept soundly, she had a strange dream. She was running through the woods in her nightgown and barefoot. The soft grass tickled her toes, and small rocks stung her soles. Suddenly, she looked down at her hands. They were covered with blood. She ran to the hollow old oak tree, where the puppy was waiting for her. Her face felt funny, and when she touched her cheeks, they were covered with fur.

Emily awoke the next morning with her heart pounding.

"What's wrong, dear?" her mother asked when Emily came down to breakfast. "You look so pale! Are you ill?"

"No," Emily shook her head. "I just had a funny dream." But she ate almost nothing, and her mother reached over to feel her forehead.

"No fever. Still, perhaps you'd better go back to bed, Emily. If you're not feeling better in an hour or two, I'll send for Dr. Jameson."

"I'm all right, Mama. Really." Emily stood up. "I think I just need some fresh air. May I be excused?"

Her mother nodded. "All right, honey. But promise me you'll go lie down if you feel badly."

"I will," Emily assured her. Then she beat a quick path to the cows, where she stole some milk and hurried on to the barn.

The bay colt, always friendly, bolted when she came in and shied away from her, refusing the lump of sugar she always brought with her. Bewildered, Emily ran to the puppy with the milk. He gulped it down.

Within a few weeks, the puppy was sleek and happy. He loved to explore, he loved Emily, but most of all, he loved meat. No longer interested in milk, he would tear into raw meat, devouring it in the blink of an eye.

One morning when Emily brought the puppy his breakfast, she was horrified to find bits and pieces of a sheep at the edge of the puppy's box. Internal organs were strewn about, and blood was everywhere. Figuring one of the farm's hounds must have brought food to the puppy, Emily cleaned up the mess and found a larger box for her fast-growing pet. Then she carried him up to a new hiding place in the hayloft.

She was just coming down from the hayloft when Owen came through the door.

"How's he doing?" Owen wanted to know.

"He's growing into a fine dog, just like I knew he would," Emily replied, trying to keep Owen from coming into the barn.

"Let's see him," Owen said and tried to push past her. But she stopped him.

"He's not here," she lied. "I found him a new hiding place."

"Where?"

"It's a secret . . . for now. In another couple of weeks, I'll take him walking and bring him over to see you," Emily promised Owen. "I just know that when Mama and Papa see what a pretty dog he is, they will let me keep him."

"You're sure acting funny," Owen muttered. But he was so infatuated with Emily that he always obeyed her.

That evening at dinner, Emily's father had disturbing news. "Two of Morgan's sheep are dead," he announced.

"Oh, no!" Mrs. Burt exclaimed. "How?"

"Morgan says it's the other wolf. They live in pairs. He shot the one, but this one's smarter. It slipped by the dogs and herded the sheep into the woods, where it slaughtered them. It can cut a sheep from the flock and do it without making a sound. And it's making off with pieces of its prey."

Emily thought of the sheep parts she had found at the puppy's box. Her heart raced, and she felt dizzy.

"We'll most likely organize a hunting party by lantern light," Mr. Burt went on. "And if there's a litter, we'll have to find it as well."

Mr. Burt looked at his daughter, as if he were waiting for her to say something.

Emily looked down at her plate. Had Owen told her father about the wolf pup in the tree hollow? Had he betrayed her?

"I'm not hungry," Emily said. "Not after that story. Sheep parts. Ugh! May I be excused?"

"Are you sure you're all right?" Her mother looked worried. "She was very pale this morning and ate no breakfast," she said to her husband.

"Yes, Mama. But I'm really tired. I think I'll turn in early."

Emily felt the urge to wear her locket to bed. In the darkness, she held it to her heart and felt closer than ever to her puppy.

That night there was a terrible storm. Thunder crashed and lightning split the sky. Emily dreamed she heard the puppy crying and that she rushed to the hayloft, barefoot and clad only in her nightie, to comfort him.

The storm woke her parents. Mrs. Burt got up to close the windows and check the doors. When she went into Emily's room, she was shocked to find an empty bed. Then she heard the back door slam and footsteps coming up the stairs. She screamed for her husband as Emily entered the room. Emily stood there, dripping wet in her nightgown, her bare feet leaving a muddy trail.

"In the name of Our Lord, where have you been?" gasped her mother.

"The barn door was banging in the storm and the horses were making such a noise, it woke me up. So I went out to make sure they didn't get loose." Emily delivered this information as though it were the most logical explanation in the world.

Mrs. Burt stared at her daughter. "In your nightclothes? With no shoes on? Why would you do such a thing?"

Emily shrugged. She was more interested in the fact that although it was very dark, except for her mother's small lighted lamp, she could see exceptionally clearly. In fact, it seemed as clear as day to her.

The following evening, Emily came in from the barn to find Owen sitting in the parlor with her father. As the boy rose to leave, Mr. Burt turned to his daughter.

"Sit down, Emily," he said.

Emily sat down. Owen didn't look at her as he went out the door.

"Another sheep was killed last night."

Emily looked down at her hands. "That's awful," she replied. Then she looked up at her father. "Papa, what was Owen doing here?"

"His father sent him. Apparently, Owen had a secret and it was time to divulge it. He says you've been hiding a baby wolf. That he found it in a hollow tree and showed it to you, and you made him promise not to tell anyone."

"It's not a wolf!" Emily cried. "It's a puppy. The sweetest little puppy you ever saw. I was hoping that, as it grew and everyone could see it was a dog, you and Mama would let me keep it."

"Show me where you're hiding it."

"No!" Emily jumped up. "He's mine! I won't let you kill him!"

She ran out the door before her father could stop her and raced into the woods. When she reached the hollow oak tree, she sank down beside it and sobbed until she fell asleep.

When she awoke, the moon was hanging like a round lantern in the sky. She could see so clearly, it was almost as though she could peer into the secret chambers of nature, witnessing hidden wonders, from the birds huddled in their nests on the highest branches of the trees to the smallest insects bustling under the rocks and leaves. And she could hear, more sharply than human ears should, footsteps a mile or two away and the soft panting of dogs just as far off.

She began to run easily, noiselessly, as though she were flying. Her hair fell into her eyes, her pulse raced, and she felt like a huge bird, leaving the earth.

Armed with guns, a wolf hunting party, Mr. Burt and Owen among them, crouched in the trees at the edge of the sheep pasture, waiting for their sneaky nocturnal quarry. Suddenly, Owen thought he saw a sheep rolling on the ground, away from the herd. His gun poised, the boy stepped silently out of the trees as a hunched animal ran past him. He fired. The creature stumbled and then disappeared, howling.

The men came running and shouting. "Where is it? Where is it?" they yelled.

But the only thing they found was blood on the ground. That damned crafty beast had gotten away!

When Mr. Burt returned home, his wife met him at the door.

"Oh, John, there's been a terrible accident," she cried. "Emily . . . she's been shot!"

A chill went through John Burt, but he wondered why he wasn't surprised.

"We've got to get her to the doctor!" his wife said.

"No!" Burt ordered. "No."

"But why?"

"I'll explain later."

Mr. Burt went upstairs, where Emily lay on her bed. She seemed to be delirious and was talking gibberish—about wolves, and moonlight, and blood, and birds, and flowers that bloom in the darkness.

An expert at treating farm injuries, Mr. Burt gave Emily some morphine he kept on hand for emergencies and sewed up the wound in her arm.

The next day, Owen came over to inquire after Emily and to give the Burts something—Emily's silver locket. He'd found it in the yard, he said—lying about where he'd really discovered it—in the blood where the wolf had been wounded the night before.

Mr. Burt accepted the locket, no questions asked, and thanked Owen.

The official story, the one that the neighbors got, was that Emily Burt had been playing with her father's pistol when it unexpectedly went off, wounding her in the arm. Emily was secretly sent off to a doctor in Paris who specialized in the psychological disorder of lycanthropy—the delusion of being a werewolf. The official story—the one the neighbors got—was that she was just fine and visiting family in Philadelphia.

A year later, Emily returned to the family's plantation in Talbot County, Georgia, where she lived out the rest of her days. A spinster until her death in 1911, at the age of seventy, she was known to be a bit of an eccentric and to lavish her affection on an odd pet dog that some said was really a wolf. Emily Burt was buried wearing the silver locket she'd received on her twelfth birthday. You can visit her grave in her family's cemetery along Jeff Hendrix Road in Belleview, Georgia.

But is Emily Burt at rest? Some say that when the moon is full and hanging like a round lantern in the night sky, a beautiful ghost wolf, sleek and silvery white in the moonlight, prowls the cemetery, evaporating with the first rays of dawn. It may be so. Who knows?

Chapter 14

The Wolf
Guardian Angel

Guardian angels can come in any form. But whoever heard of one in the form of a wolf? In the following story, a young girl is visited by a ghost wolf—why, she has no idea. But it seems this odd presence is benign and, incredibly enough, concerned with her welfare.

When Delia was a little girl, she often spent the night at her grandparents' house on the Southern California coast—a beautiful, sixties Art Deco estate on a hilltop overlooking the ocean. On a clear day, you could see forever—or at least out to Catalina Island. At night, because there were so few houses and street lights in the area, you had a panoramic view of all the stars in the sky.

Delia loved nature, and plenty of natural beauty surrounded that house. The yards were large and full of interesting vegetation, and the indigenous landscape beyond was lush with many trees and an abundance of wildflowers. In addition, Delia's grandparents kept birdhouses and bird feeders on every porch, and there were several large stone birdbaths on the property. Delia enjoyed watching the many feathered species that were always around, eagerly partaking of food, water, and shelter.

One of the home's more intriguing features was a spacious atrium built in the center of the house. This large circular room had a completely open ceiling that allowed the birds to fly in and out, a dirt floor covered with rocks and gravel, and, of course, a birdbath and feeder. Instead of walls, there were huge glass windows and sliding glass doors. When the curtains were open, you could see straight through the living room into the two guest bedrooms, one of which was Delia's.

Delia adored her grandparents, but she had mixed feelings about the house. Despite its spaciousness, fascinating objets d'art, and the comforting presence of family photos on the shelves and along the walls, it was not what you'd call homey. Delia's grandparents almost never entertained, preferring to go out to restaurants, concerts, and the theater with their friends. In all the time she spent there, Delia could not recall one visitor coming over. But what really bothered her was the nagging feeling of being watched.

"There was a sort of eerie feeling that I always got when I stayed there," she mused. "I was very sensitive to energies, although I didn't understand what that meant at the time. I wasn't afraid of ghosts, because I wasn't allowed to watch horror movies, so I thought that if there were such things as ghosts, they were cute and friendly, like Casper.

"Nevertheless, I always had a sense of discomfort in that house, and often I'd cry and call my parents, begging them to come and get me. It just seemed like there were invisible entities around, watching me."

One night, Delia couldn't sleep. She lay awake in the dark, staring at the display of handmade dolls her grandmother kept on the dresser across from the bed. They were all intriguing, from various countries and cultures, and each seemed to have a story to tell. The only thing on the dresser that disturbed her was a stuffed animal, a coyote that seemed somewhat rudely out of place among the dolls.

"I used to sleep with stuffed animals, but I was eleven and figured I was too old for that sort of thing. But that coyote freaked me out, with its lolling tongue and big, white eyes," Delia said. "However, I couldn't keep my eyes off the dolls. I stared at them for hours, unable to relax."

On this particular night, her grandmother had forgotten to close the curtains between the atrium and Delia's room. Although there was no moon, Delia could see straight into the atrium. For some inexplicable reason, the big, dark room filled her with fear. The sky looked black and starless through the open ceiling, almost like a black hole that would swallow her up if she gazed too long at it.

"I wanted to get up and close the curtains, but I was too scared," she recalled. "Finally, I felt so restless that I decided to get up, close the curtains, and watch the TV with no sound, so as not to disturb my grandparents, until I was sleepy enough to go back to bed."

Delia looked up, and through the glass, she saw the distinct image of a ghostly woman in a long white dress. The figure was sitting on the edge of the birdbath, combing her hair with her fingers. She was exquisitely beautiful, with long, honey-colored hair. Her delicate, slender feet were bare, and she had an almost wistful expression as she ran her fingers through her thick, luxurious tresses. She seemed to be completely unaware of Delia's presence.

Delia was both petrified and mesmerized. "Somehow, in spite of the chilly fear that I felt because I could see the stone edges of the birdbath through her, I felt a little sad for her. She seemed like she was waiting for someone or something that would never come. I sat there for a few minutes watching her, my heart pounding and my palms sweating. I could barely feel myself breathing."

Suddenly, Delia saw two bright red pinpoints of light on the other side of the glass in the living room. "I looked past the woman and saw a huge black wolf with its upper lip curling in an angry snarl. It had jagged black teeth, and the two red pinpoints of light were its eyes. But it didn't seem to notice me. It was looking at the ghost woman, and its fur was standing on end."

As Delia watched in disbelief, the entire affair took on a theatrical aspect. It seemed as if the two characters were playing a scene. The woman stood up and turned to face the wolf as if in some sort of standoff. Then she vanished. The wolf turned its gaze on Delia, but it was no longer menacing. Then it, too, disappeared.

Delia lost no time racing into her grandparents' room and jumping into bed with them. She struggled to tell them what had just happened, but she was so excited and terrified that her grandmother had to calm her down before the words could make their way out. Her grandparents were mystified, as neither of them had ever seen a ghost, and they thought that perhaps tiredness coupled with the atrium's strange reflections might have caused Delia to hallucinate.

Delia stopped her overnight visits to her grandparents and did not return to the house until she was sixteen. Although she spent the night, she made sure the curtains were closed and didn't fall asleep until daybreak.

She often thought about the ghost wolf and the possibility that he might have been protecting her.

When Delia was in her early twenties, she had an asthma attack while hiking in the San Gabriel Mountains outside of Los Angeles.

"I had fallen behind the other two girls I was with, and it was very hot. I began to gasp for breath and realized I didn't have my inhaler with me. Panic caused my chest to close up even more. Suddenly, I saw the wolf step out of thin air between two trees. He stared at me, and I saw that his eyes were chocolate brown, not red. As I stared back at him, I could feel myself taking deeper, slower breaths. It felt like he was telling me to calm down. He stood there, watching over me as if to make sure I was going to be all right. I felt safe in his presence and was able to relax enough so that the attack passed. When I could breathe again, the wolf disappeared back into the trees."

What might have been the significance of this wolf spirit in Delia's life? He was obviously a protector of some sort; perhaps there was also a lesson she was supposed to learn from him.

In many Native American tribes, the wolf is considered to be the highest spiritual teacher, even above the hawk and eagle. Wolves are fiercely loyal and protective, and their "medicine" can help in the attainment of self-confidence, success, courage, and spiritual insight. According to Native American legends, the color of the wolf determines the lesson or knowledge it brings. The red wolf, for instance, is a symbol of power both physical and mystical, associated with the red "wolf star," Sirius. Red wolf medicine, it's said, brings strength, speed, courage, and spiritual insight.

Who's afraid of the big, bad wolf? Not Delia. To her, he's the guardian angel who saved her life.

Chapter 15

The Witch and
the Blackbird

"Ther's very few bu' what un heard,
In Burslem straights a ghost appeared,
Bu' if yo 'anner heerd this teel,
What makes the staughtest mon turn peel,
Just pae attention unta mae,
Oi'l tell yo aw abait Molly Leigh."
—Old Staffordshire rhyme

There's hardly a resident of North Staffordshire, England, who isn't familiar with the legend of Molly Leigh, otherwise known as the Burslem witch. For centuries, children have grown up singing, "Molly Leigh, Molly Leigh, follow me, follow me! Molly Leigh, Molly Leigh, can't catch me!" as they run around her large, cracked headstone in St. John's churchyard. It's an exhilarating game spiked with a delicious hint of terror; if you've got the nerve to recite the verse three times in a row, the witch just might rise up out of her grave and come after you!

The story of Molly Leigh begins in 1685, when she was born Margaret Leigh in the small country town of Burslem, near the city of Stoke-on-Trent, an austere area surrounded by the bleak Staffordshire Moorlands—the perfect breeding ground for a witch. From birth, Molly exhibited a chilling strangeness. She suckled on animals, they said. She chewed on stale bread even before her teeth came in. She was an uncommonly unattractive child, with a long nose, crooked teeth, and small black eyes that reminded one of a furtive animal. She was even said to be humpbacked.

The unfortunate girl had no friends, save the animals on the Leigh farm. Her homeliness and the rumors surrounding her made people afraid of her. Whenever she went into town, all who saw her would cross themselves and turn away, lest they be cursed with the evil eye.

When Molly was sixteen, her parents died, leaving her completely alone and isolated. She kept the cows and scraped out a meager living delivering milk. When she walked the Burslem streets hawking her wares, her ugly face set in a perennial frown and her pet blackbird perched on her shoulder, she was, indeed, a creepy sight to behold.

Rumors were always circulating about Molly Leigh. Whether they were true was of little consequence; the townsfolk had already branded her an outcast and were inclined to believe anything negative about her. The first rumor was that she sold bad milk. Now, a soured batch or two was inevitable in that era when pasteurization and refrigeration had yet to be invented. But Molly also was accused of watering down the milk, an offense that could instantly put her out of business.

Then, an even more destructive rumor about Molly arose: that she was a witch. Who else would have a blackbird for a pet? It was obviously her "familiar"—an animal with magical powers that a witch will take as her constant companion and confidant. Travelers going along the road past Molly's small farm reported that the hawthorn bush outside her cottage, which was the bird's favorite perch, never blossomed. The townspeople were convinced that the creature was an omen of misfortune and death.

Reverend Spencer, the rector of St. John's Church, stoked the fires of suspicion. He publicly proclaimed that he had never seen Molly in church. In the ultra-pious seventeenth century, that was a sin of monumental proportions.

The story goes that when Molly heard of the Reverend's claim, she grew so angry that she swore vengeance. She sent her blackbird to spy on the clergyman at his favorite drinking spot, the Turk's Head. When the bird perched atop the pub sign, the beer turned sour, and the patrons were suddenly struck with rheumatism so painful that their howls could be heard all the way to the next county!

The Reverend rose to the occasion. He grabbed his gun and shot the blackbird. But he missed. The bird flew off squawking, and the Reverend took to his bed with terrible, mysterious stomach pains that lasted for weeks.

A superstitious fervor overtook Burslem. Molly became a total pariah. She was blamed for any and all misfortunes and was basically run out of town. The beleaguered woman retreated to the country, to live out her days in lonely solitude with the cows and her blackbird as her only friends. She died in 1748, at the then old age of sixty-three.

But instead of the rumors being laid to rest along with Molly, it seemed they were just beginning to really heat up. Legend has it that she was no sooner six feet under than a party led by Reverend Spencer went to her cottage in search of the malevolent blackbird. When they peered through the grimy windows, they saw no bird, but they did see Molly, rocking by the fire and muttering a weird sort of chant: "Weight and measure sold I never! Milk and water sold I never!"

This threw Burslem into a tizzy. Was the curse of the undead upon them? Had they gotten on the wrong side of a witch far more powerful than they'd ever imagined? Would Molly haunt them forever and take her revenge on each and every one of them?

As if to verify their fears, the nefarious blackbird became a fixture in town, swooping down upon people, pecking them, and otherwise harassing them with ceaseless crowing day and night. It seemed as though he were taunting his mistress's tormentors and had been sent from Hell as a constant reminder of their foolhardy cruelty.

The townspeople were at their wits' end. They had tried everything in their power to get rid of the blackbird. They swatted at it with brooms and rakes. They threw rocks and stones at it. They took bows and arrows and guns to it. But nothing could touch the fiendish pest.

Finally, Reverend Spencer decided to appeal to the only power greater than Satan. He summoned together a group of local priests. One moonless midnight in April, the clerics made their way to St. John's churchyard carrying shovels and a mysterious sack, which was bouncing and thrashing about as if possessed.

At Molly's grave, they set to work, digging until they reached the casket, whereupon they exhumed the body. Then, accompanied by the appropriate prayers, they drove a stake through the dead woman's heart. It was said that upon being pierced, a horrible cry burst forth from the corpse, and the moon appeared in the sky, flooding the scene with light.

The priests then grabbed something from the sack. It was the blackbird, flapping its wings and trying vainly to screech through a sock that had been wrapped tightly around its beak. How they managed to catch the bird is unknown, but why they hadn't killed it is. According to an old antidote to witchcraft, after the stake is driven through the witch's heart, she must be returned to her coffin with her familiar, who must be buried alive alongside her. So, duly informed, the priests returned Molly's corpse to the casket and bundled the bird in with her, after which they hastily resealed the lid and reinterred the deadly duo.

The ritual seemed to work. The witch of Burslem never again bothered the town. But some people say that late at night, on the anniversary of Molly Leigh's death, a faint cawing can be heard on the wings of the wind. Others claim that the blackbird can still be seen in ghostly form, sitting on his owner's tombstone as if keeping watch over her, like any faithful pet.

One nagging question, however, has never been answered. If Molly Leigh were really a witch, why was she laid to rest in the churchyard, with Reverend Spencer himself performing the ceremony? No witch would ever have been buried in consecrated ground.

Today, Molly Leigh's grave is Staffordshire's most popular tourist attraction, and on Halloween, adults and children alike circle it while chanting the old dare:

"Molly Leigh, Molly Leigh,
Follow me! Follow me!
Molly Leigh, Molly Leigh,
Catch me if you can!"

Chapter 16

Rescued by a
Ghost Pet

Some of the most fascinating paranormal cases involving animals center around deceased pets appearing to their owners in times of crisis to warn them of imminent danger or to guide them to safety— just as they undoubtedly would have in life. What magnificent beings our pets are—loyal and devoted to and beyond the end, putting our welfare above everything and shattering the barrier between the worlds of earth and spirit to continue to look out for us.

At the end of World War II, a soldier named Joe was returning to his family in Virginia's Shenandoah Valley. When Joe got off the train, he was still a few miles from his destination and had to walk the rest of the way home. He didn't mind, as he was thrilled to be back in the beautiful Virginia countryside. But it was growing dark, so he walked as fast as he could on the road along the river until he reached the area where he had to cross over to the other side.

There were two bridges: the older, girder-type bridge that he remembered and a new one that had been erected during his absence. Joe decided to use the new bridge, which was closer and probably safer, he reasoned. Just as he was about to step onto the bridge, he heard barking in the distance. Turning around, he saw a dog racing toward him. He could barely make the figure out in the dusk. But as it grew nearer, he gave a shout. It was their old family dog, Shep!

"Shep!" he cried. "How did you know to find me here, old buddy?"

The dog jumped up on him, whining ecstatically, and Joe hugged him tightly.

"Boy, did I miss you!" he whispered, burying his face in Shep's shaggy fur. "Come on, boy, let's go. I'm so excited to see everybody, I'm about to burst."

But when Joe started across the bridge, Shep stopped and began barking again.

"What's the matter, boy?" Joe felt himself growing impatient. "Come on, now. I'll race you home."

But Shep began tugging at Joe's pants leg. When Joe tried to shake him off, the dog grabbed the young soldier's ankle in his teeth and gently bit him. By this time, Joe understood that, for some strange reason, Shep did not want him to take this particular route home.

"Okay, general, which way?" he laughed, saluting the dog.

Barking and dancing around in front of Joe, Shep led the way to the other bridge. Joe was surprised when the dog raced ahead of him, eventually disappearing into the darkness. They had always walked together, and he would have thought Shep would have stuck close to him, especially after their long separation. But then he figured the animal probably wanted to get back to the family, to alert them of his arrival.

At last, he reached home. He called out to the family, and everyone came running. Amidst the shouts, hugs, and tears, Joe said, "I would have been here sooner, only Shep made me come the long way. Where is he, by the way? He ran on ahead, and I lost him."

Everyone grew silent. Then his mother said, "Shep? He was with you?"

"Yeah," Joe laughed. "I couldn't believe it when he showed up. That dog sure has a sixth sense."

Joe's mother, father, and sister exchanged glances. Then his dad said gently, "Son, Shep died last winter. We didn't write you about it because we didn't want to upset you."

The next morning, Joe learned that the river, which had risen with the spring rains, had flooded the new bridge and taken out the middle section. If he had tried to cross it in the dark that night, he would surely have drowned. He knew then that Shep had come back from the next world "on leave" to save his life.

✛

Then there is the story of Smudge, a little stray who came into the lives of Marilyn Peters and her son, Jake, just when they needed him.

Marilyn was a single mother. She and ten-year-old Jake lived in a run-down apartment building on the edge of a rural town, which was, unfortunately, a dumping ground for unwanted animals from a nearby large city. The farms had a surplus of barn cats and farm dogs, and strays were everywhere.

Marilyn and Jake loved cats, but their landlord didn't allow pets. In fact, he hated animals, and rumor linked him to the mysterious disappearance of several neighborhood pets. Somehow, though, the strays always managed to find Marilyn.

"The cats know you're a softie, Mom," Jake teased her. "They can smell you a mile away."

Marilyn laughed. Jake was right. Skinny, scruffy cats and kittens were always showing up on their porch, where they were sure to find a square meal and plenty of love.

But because of the landlord, who liked to brag that he kept plenty of poison and buckshot on hand to deal with stray cats and dogs, Marilyn was careful never to let them into the apartment.

One night a stray black cat showed up at their apartment. Jake immediately recognized the animal.

"He hangs around that old abandoned house at the end of the road," he told his mother. "Probably someone dumped him."

They fed the cat, and he cozied up to them, happy as could be. The tom was definitely a man about town, however, and would disappear during the day, returning in the evening for his dinner and a good old stroking session. When he would come limping in after a fight, Marilyn would clean his wounds and pull the burrs out of his sleek fur. The cat was always appreciative, purring and rubbing against them, and it wasn't long before Marilyn and Jake became hopelessly attached to him.

Jake named him Smudge and bought him a bright neon-pink nylon collar. He wrote "Smudge" on the collar with a bright green permanent marker and put it on the cat. Smudge seemed very proud of his splendid collar and strutted around like a real gentleman.

They all got into a comfortable routine. Smudge would disappear during the day, and when it got dark, Marilyn and Jake would hear his little meow and his scratching on the screen door. If they were gone, Smudge would wait patiently on their porch until they came home. Then he'd rub up against them, get his dinner, stay for some loving, and depart. This went on for several months, until Marilyn was forced to move from the apartment and in with her sister and brother-in-law to cut expenses.

Jake begged to take Smudge with them, but Marilyn was firm.

"I understand how you feel, sweetheart, because I feel the same way," she said as she hugged her son. "You know I'd bring him with us if it were at all possible. But we're imposing enough on Aunt Chris and Uncle Ed. We simply can't spring a pet on them, too."

One night a couple of days before the move, Smudge didn't show up for his nightly visit. Nor did Marilyn and Jake hear his familiar meow and scratching the next night or the night after that. With heavy hearts, they loaded the moving van. Then Marilyn lit a match to the stove, which had never worked properly, and put a pizza in the oven, thinking that it would be their last dinner in the dingy apartment and how nice it would be to finally be able to cook on a decent stove. While the pizza was baking, she and Jake sat down to take a breather and play some cards. Suddenly, they heard the telltale scratching at the screen door.

"Smudge!" Jake shouted and raced to the door.

Sure enough, there was the errant feline. Jake picked him up and nuzzled him, and Smudge purred his little cat heart out. Marilyn came out to the porch, and as the three of them were having a great big cuddle, a bright light flashed from the kitchen and the gas oven exploded.

The fire department rushed to the scene, sirens screaming. After they'd put out the fire, one of the firemen shook his head.

"That stove was an accident waiting to happen," he said. "You're awfully lucky you were outside when it blew, ma'am. If you'd been in that kitchen, you might not be alive."

Marilyn was thoroughly shaken. The kitchen table was burned to a crisp. She shuddered at the thought that just a few moments before, she and Jake had been sitting at that table . . . until Smudge had arrived and called them out to the porch. She went over to Jake, who was standing nearby in a frightened daze clutching the cat, who seemed perfectly content in his arms.

"How can we ever thank you, Smudge?" she said, stroking their savior, who merely responded with a happy purr. That's when it hit her. While they were packing, she'd found an old pet carrier in the closet and, for some reason, she'd thrown it in the truck. Now she knew why.

"We're taking Smudge with us," Marilyn told Jake, who broke into a joyful laugh.

Marilyn got the carrier out of the truck, and Smudge obediently climbed into it. Since their remaining few belongings had been destroyed in the fire, she decided they might as well leave then and there. With Jake grinning in the front seat and Smudge purring in the carrier, Marilyn drove out of the driveway and down the road to the stop sign at the intersection with the highway.

As they were waiting at the intersection, Marilyn saw something out of the corner of her eye that made her blood run cold. On the side of the road was a little black cat that had obviously been run over. She pulled over as soon as she could, and telling Jake to stay in the truck, she got out and ran over to the lifeless body. She could tell it had been there for a few days, because it was already starting to decay. Then she let out a cry. Around the dead cat's neck was a bright pink collar with the letters S-M-U-D-G-E written in Jake's uneven hand.

Marilyn stood there in disbelief. How? How could Smudge be lying here dead when he was inside the truck in the carrier?

But when Marilyn got back in the truck and checked the carrier, it was empty.

"We firmly believe that Smudge came back to save our lives and then went his final way," Marilyn said. "One last nightly visit."

✛

One of the most perplexing accounts of a phantom pet rescue mission took place some 150 years ago.

From the bay window of his comfortable house on a hill in the Missouri countryside, Dr. John O'Brien gazed out at the whirling blizzard. He hoped they had enough wood and essentials to get them through the storm. He and his wife would be virtual prisoners in their home for the next few days or even, God forbid, weeks, snowed in until the weather eased up and the hard work of shoveling themselves out could begin. Neighbors were few and far between; the nearest house was at least two miles away. If a man chose the country life, he soon learned the art of making do for himself.

The snow danced in the moonlight, spinning a web of silver lace on the windowpane. Marveling at nature's dual character, the doctor rose, lit another lantern, and put another log on the fire. It was six o'clock, and his young wife, Elizabeth, was just getting dinner on the table.

"It's surely a night to hunker down, isn't it?" she smiled.

John just nodded. He was thinking about his cursed intuition, which had chosen this moment to kick in and tell him that one of his patients, old Mrs. Kilpatrick, wasn't doing well.

How would he know that? This was the age before telephones, and no messenger had come to relay the news. But all the same, the young doctor had a feeling—and his feelings had yet to be wrong.

As they sat down to eat, Elizabeth couldn't help but notice how preoccupied her husband seemed. "What is it, John?" she asked. "You act as though this is the Last Supper."

"I hope to God it isn't. Listen, Lizzie, you know Mrs. Kilpatrick?"

"The woman with the heart condition?"

"Yes. Well, I haven't checked up on her for quite some time, and I . . ."

"And you've got one of your 'feelings.'"

"You know me too well," he laughed, reaching over and patting her hand.

"But John, the Kilpatricks live four miles away. You can't possibly mean to go out there in this storm! Why, you can't see your hand in front of your face, let alone the road. And besides . . ." she reached over and put her hand on his strong arm, "tomorrow's Christmas Eve."

"I know, love. I'll be back by then, I promise," John assured her. "Old Jack will find the way. I don't know what I'd do without that horse. He's really the driver, not me. Many's the scrapes he's pulled us out of. He'll get us there and home again in one piece, don't you worry."

"John, you know I understand," she tried to reason with him. "Your caring nature is the reason I married you, after all. But sometimes you care too much for others, and not enough for yourself. If anything happens to you tonight, what will become of all those who depend on you? I don't mean me; I took this job for better or worse. But all your patients, including Mrs. Kilpatrick. Can't you wait until morning, at least? The snow might stop by then."

"I wish I could," he replied. "But that damn feeling won't let me. It's saying morning will be too late. I've got to go now, Lizzie."

Rising from the table, he took her in his arms, kissed her, and proceeded to put on his heavy overcoat, cap, fur-lined gloves, and thick woolen muffler.

"I may spend the night there, so don't wait up." He blew Elizabeth a parting kiss.

"You know I will," she replied.

The doctor trudged out to the stable and hitched Jack to the buggy. He loaded his bag onto the box spring seat and climbed in. The horse whinnied nervously and pawed the deep snow.

"Easy, fellow," John soothed him. "This isn't the first snowstorm you've ever seen."

He took one last look over his shoulder, hoping to see Elizabeth's face at the window, but he could barely make out the house. Then he jerked the reins, and they were off down the road, which was no longer visible under the thick drifts.

The blinding snow stung the doctor's face, and he looked in vain for the turn he had to take, the blizzard having wiped out familiar landmarks. His heart sinking, he was about to turn around and try to make it home when he heard, through the howling wind, what he thought was a barking dog. Was he imagining things? No, he heard it again, this time louder. Shielding his eyes with one hand and gripping the reins with the other, he peered through the swirling snow, trying to make out something, anything. Then, out of nowhere, it seemed, two giant mastiffs appeared, flanking his horse.

It was the most bizarre sight. Where had the huge dogs come from? Why would they be out in the storm? Dr. O'Brien searched his memory. He knew all the families in the area, and no one, to his knowledge, owned such beasts.

But the strangest thing of all was how the dogs were standing there, barking like mad, as if they had to have his attention. Then, they began to run just ahead of old Jack, looking back over their shoulders and barking, as if to say, "This way! Follow us!"

Another "feeling" overtook the doctor—the inner certainty that the dogs were there to lead him to his destination. Slowly, the horse and buggy ground their way through the snow, the doctor faithfully following the dogs' lead. When they turned, he turned; if the buggy lagged behind, the dogs stopped and waited patiently, barking to assure the doctor of their presence.

Finally, the frozen and exhausted doctor made out a light in the distance. As he drew closer, he saw, with unutterable relief, that it was a lantern in the window of the Kilpatrick house. Parking his rig in the shed next to the house, he grabbed his bag and pounded at the door. Joseph Kilpatrick let him in, looking dumbfounded.

"Doctor O'Brien! What are you doing here?"

"I had a feeling, Joe, that the missus wasn't doing well," he explained, wet and shaking.

"Praise be to God, your feeling was right. She's having terrible trouble with her breathing, and her pulse is awful low. Bless you for coming out in this dirty weather."

Removing his soaking, icy overcoat and gloves, the doctor warmed his hands briefly by the fire. Then he went into the bedroom. The sound of Mrs. Kilpatrick's labored breathing filled the room.

"How are you, Mrs. Kilpatrick?" the doctor asked, taking her wrist and checking her pulse.

The sick woman struggled to open her eyes. "Is that you, Dr. O'Brien?" she gasped.

"Yes, dear, it's me. Just take it easy. Your pulse is pretty low, but I've got some medicine here for your heart that I think is going to do the trick."

"Doctor . . ." Mrs. Kilpatrick seemed to have something urgent to impart. "I saw you . . . I dreamed I saw you . . ."

"That's good, Mrs. Kilpatrick. Now don't try to talk."

". . . driving through the storm . . . with two great beasts . . ."

Dr. O'Brien leaned over his patient. "What, Mrs. Kilpatrick? What did you say?"

". . . dogs the like of which I've never seen."

She sank back on the pillow. Dr. O'Brien quickly administered a dose of the medication.

"There now, Mrs. Kilpatrick. This will help your breathing. Just relax and go to sleep."

When Mrs. Kilpatrick's breathing grew easier and she had fallen into a deep sleep, the doctor turned to her husband.

"She'll be all right now, Joe. Give her a spoonful of this every couple of hours," the good doctor instructed. "And now, I could use a bit of medicine myself. You wouldn't happen to have any brandy around, would you?"

"From one Irishman to another, and why wouldn't I?" Joe Kilpatrick put his arm around the doctor, and together the two men went into the parlor.

Over brandy, bread, and meat, they chatted by the fire, though Dr. O'Brien kept thinking about Mrs. Kilpatrick's eerie statement. Suddenly he realized that he hadn't heard the barking dogs since he arrived.

"Tell me, Joe, where are those dogs of yours?" he asked.

"Dogs?" Joe Kilpatrick was perplexed. "I don't have any dogs, doctor. Why would you ask that?"

The young doctor then told his host about his strange experience.

"That's a mystery, all right," Joe nodded. "Nobody around here owns such animals."

Then O'Brien told Joe about Mrs. Kilpatrick's dream.

"I've got the chills now," Joe replied, reaching for the brandy. "Surely, this is the doing of angels."

The doctor nodded. He felt peaceful and extremely sleepy. Within minutes, he was snoring softly in his chair. When he awoke, it was dawn and the storm had lifted.

As he drove home that morning, he looked everywhere for the dogs. He even whistled and called them. But all was as silent as the snow that glistened in the sunrise.

During the next few days, the doctor inquired all around, asking everyone he knew about the mastiffs. But no one had ever seen such animals in the area.

Realizing that the great beasts had vanished as abruptly as they had appeared, Dr. O'Brien finally had to conclude that his guides on that bitter, stormy night had been spirit helpers, sent from somewhere beyond the earth to come to his and Mrs. Kilpatrick's rescue. Joe Kilpatrick was right: It must have been the doing of the angels on their Christmas rounds.

Chapter 17

Reincarnated Pets

Can pets reincarnate? Well, if you believe that your pet has a soul, then why not? There are numerous accounts of a pet passing on and seeming to reappear in another animal's body. In the psychic world, this is known as a "walk in." The departed soul enters someone else's body, and the "possessed" person assumes the characteristics and personality of the dead person. The same phenomenon apparently occurs in the animal world, as the following stories prove.

When Troy Norman was twelve, his mother brought home a kitten that her coworker had given her. The new arrival was named Otto, and for both Troy and the cat, it was love at first sight.

"He immediately became attached to me," Troy recalled. "He was an absolute joy—sweet tempered, incredibly affectionate, and playful even as an adult. Otto was a born entertainer and was always doing funny and unexpected things that made us laugh."

When Troy was twenty, he married and moved into an apartment where animals weren't allowed. Troy had a hard time saying goodbye to his best friend. But the new apartment wasn't far from his parents, and when Troy's first child was born, his mother was chief babysitter. So Troy saw Otto frequently. The cat also forged a close bond with Troy's young son, Timmy.

Several years later, at the age of sixteen, Otto grew sick. When his condition deteriorated to the point that the vet could do no more for him, Troy's parents made the heart-wrenching decision to have the old cat put to sleep. Troy accompanied his dad to the vet, and held Otto in his arms until it was all over.

"It was one of the hardest things I've ever had to do," he remembered.

Timmy, who was five at the time, was devastated.

Five years went by, and still Troy missed Otto. He told himself that the cat had had a good long life, full of love, and that there was nothing to grieve. But we never stop missing those we've loved and lost. Otto had left a hole in Troy's heart that was too big for any other animal to fill . . . until his cousin's cat gave birth to kittens, one of which bore an eerie resemblance to Otto.

"He had the same markings," said Troy. "A pretty silver gray, with a white blaze up his nose and forehead and white paws. The tip of Otto's tail looked like it had been dipped in white paint, and this kitten had the same distinguishing feature."

Although all the kittens were adorable, Troy felt drawn to the one that resembled his childhood pet. "I thought I'd never get another cat after Otto died," Troy said. "But I had this odd, overwhelming desire to take him home."

When the kitten was twelve weeks old, Troy adopted him. To his astonishment, the kitten exhibited behaviors so similar to Otto's that he had the unshakable feeling his old cat had returned. When trying to decide on a name for the little fellow, Otto Two was the only one he thought of. It didn't seem at all like he was replacing his old friend; it just seemed perfectly natural.

"Otto Two began doing things just the way Otto One did," Troy said. "For instance, the old Otto had this habit of nipping my heel to get my attention. Otto Two did the same thing. Otto One had a quirky affinity for asparagus; so did Otto Two. It went on and on.

"It might sound crazy, but Otto Two will look into my eyes like he knows me. I have absolutely no doubt that our old Otto is back, and it's the greatest feeling in the world."

⌖

I totally believe Troy's story, because the same thing happened to me.

I've had umpteen cats in my life, but none as close to me as Petie. He was one of a litter of five that my young cat, Angel, gave birth to on my bed. From the very first, Petie was my boy. He had a calm, loving energy, and of all the kittens, he was the one who grew most attached to me.

Petie was the shyest of the litter, the one the others would push around. When the kittens were feeding, he was the last to get a teat; he'd try to worm his way in, but the others always pushed him away, and he'd wait patiently until they'd finished. When the babies were old enough to eat out of their bowls, the same thing happened. Petie would always get pushed away from his food by one of his brothers or sisters, and he would back off with a sad little mew.

I started giving him special attention and putting his food on the counter, away from the others. Then I'd lift him up, kiss him, and stick him in front of his bowl. Soon, he wouldn't eat until he got his kiss, a ritual that continued throughout his life.

Petie grew into a beautiful, long-haired cat, black and white with a white patch over one eye and a black patch over the other, which made him look like that mutt Petie in those

Little Rascals shorts. Hence, his name. He had gorgeous light green eyes that seemed to bore straight into your soul.

Petie was the brother of Rhonda Susan, whom I've talked about in a couple of chapters. But he and Rhonda couldn't have been more different. While she was always skittish, and well, let's be frank, neurotic, Petie was laid-back and steady. While Rhonda hated to be picked up and cuddled, Petie would just curl up in my arms, purring happily. But only in *my* arms. I was Petie's special person, and he was my special boy.

That cat absolutely adored me. I had never experienced such a bond with an animal. He knew what I was thinking, and he had a thoughtful intelligence that bordered on creepy. He didn't act like a cat. He acted like a noble human being, who'd somehow acquired a feline body.

Petie had a number of rituals. In addition to the kiss on the head that he demanded before his meals, he had a welcoming routine. He'd always be waiting for me in front of the house, and as soon as my car pulled into the driveway he'd flop down on the ground, purring and rolling back and forth, paws outstretched. I would squat down and rub his big, furry belly, and he'd take my hand in his paws and pull it against his chest. If my arms were full of, say groceries, I'd have to put them down and oblige him, because if I didn't, he'd meow loudly and swat at my ankle.

Another thing about Petie was that he only liked dry cat food. Every other cat I'd owned would turn its nose up at kibble if canned food or tempting morsels of people food were available. Rhonda only wanted canned food, in only certain flavors, and if she got some of my roast chicken or hot dogs or tuna—oh, happy day! But Petie would merely sniff such delicacies and wander over to his "crunchies," looking up at me for his kiss.

One day, I pulled into the driveway and Petie wasn't there to greet me. That was unusual, but I didn't give it much thought. When, however, he didn't come home that night, I grew worried. Coyotes were a real problem in Los Angeles, and there were always "Lost Cat" signs posted on trees and in the local establishments of my residential community. But Petie and Rhonda had been outdoor cats all their lives, and they'd been with me thirteen years. They were experts at fending for themselves in the wilds of L.A.

I walked the entire neighborhood calling for Petie that evening . . . and the next night, and the next, and the next. We put up signs with his photo all over. I went to the animal shelter, dreading having to check the cages of all the poor little lost souls who reached out to me through the wire openings, pawing desperately for attention and help. But Petie wasn't there.

He never came back, and though broken-hearted, I never stopped praying that one day I'd see his sweet, fuzzy face again.

Two years passed. I moved from Los Angeles to Michigan to help in the care of my elderly mother. I still had my other cat, Rhonda, and my Chihuahua, Truman. But I missed Petie something awful.

On the way to Michigan, I said a prayer: "Please, Lord, send me a stray boy cat like Petie."

About a week after I settled into my new place, I saw a skinny young kitten staring at me through the dining room window. He was white with a sprinkling of light brown that made him look like he'd been dusted with cinnamon, and he had the most amazing blue eyes I'd ever seen; they reminded me of a serene summer sky or a sun-dappled ocean. The fact that they were slightly crossed only added to the kitten's charms.

He was dirty and very thin. Those crossed blue eyes looked at me beseechingly. I grabbed a bowl and a can of cat food and ran outside. The kitten watched me tentatively. Although too afraid to approach me, he didn't run away. I filled the bowl and set it down on the ground.

"Come on, sweetie," I coaxed him.

Hunger triumphed over fear, and the kitten slowly approached the bowl. I backed away to give him space. He dug in, inhaling the food as though he hadn't eaten in days, which I'm sure he hadn't. Then he sauntered over to me and rubbed against my leg in gratitude. I reached down and gathered him up. He purred and purred and lay contentedly in my arms, just like Petie used to.

Was this scruffy young cat the answer to my prayer?

I went back into the house, the kitten still in my arms. But as soon as I opened the door and he caught sight of Truman staring jealously up at him and growling, he jumped down and ran off. But he didn't go far. He took up residence outside the house and would meow at the window, announcing his presence. I fed him outside, and even put a sign on the porch reading, "Hungry Kitty Café. All cats welcome. Please meow for service."

One day, the kitten got up the nerve to venture inside. He explored the house from top to bottom, backing off when he encountered Rhonda, who hissed and shook her tail at him, and Truman, who sniffed him and clipped his nose. I formally adopted him then and there, and named him Junior Augustus, "the last roamin' emperor."

Junior was such a sweet, loving cat that he soon won over his grumpy brother and sister. It wasn't long before

Rhonda was grooming him as she used to do with Petie. In fact, she seemed happy again, as though she had her brother back.

From the first, I'd felt an odd connection to this stray. Even though he looked nothing like Petie, he resembled him in so many other ways that I was mystified. He gazed at me like Petie used to, with that adoring intentness that seemed to peer straight into my soul. He loved to be rocked in my arms for as long as I'd hold him, hind feet sticking up in the air, front paws caressing my cheek. And he waited outside for me to come home, flopping down on the ground as soon as my car pulled into the driveway, rolling in the dirt, and reaching up for me to rub his belly. But it got weirder. He preferred dry food to canned, and he turned up his nose at people food.

One day as I filled his bowl with kibble, he looked up at me and meowed.

"What is it, Junior?" I asked.

He meowed again, butting his head against me.

"Oh, you little sweetie," I cooed, kissing him on the head . . . whereupon he turned to his bowl and dug in.

From that day on, Junior would not eat until he'd received his kiss on the head—exactly like Petie.

I couldn't help but believe that Junior was Petie reincarnated. There could be no other explanation. The similarities were simply too striking. For the first time since Petie's disappearance, I felt at peace. I kissed Junior on his soft, furry little head.

"Are you Petie?" I whispered.

He gazed up at me adoringly with those crossed blue eyes and purred his heart out.

Chapter 18
Trotty and the Headless Ghost

Anytime you're approached by a ghost, it's a good idea to have a dog with you. I put my own spin on the following legend related in Daniel Cohen's Dangerous Ghosts *about Gabe Fisher, who was walking home from the local pub late one night with his beagle, Trotty, when he heard a scream. The events that followed would forever haunt him and serve as a humbling reminder that sometimes dogs are smarter than we are.*

Gabe Fisher had had a little too much to drink.

"Hey, Gabe, you'd better put up here for the night," laughed Terry "Sure Shot" Markham, the owner of the White Bull Tavern. They called him Sure Shot because he was sure to ply you with whiskey and just as sure to take all your money. "If you reel in at this hour, your missus'll give you what for, all right!"

"Ahhh," Gabe waved away Markham's teasing with an unsteady hand. "No woman tells me when to come and go. No sir! Pour me another, Terry, old man. The night is young."

"And you're not," Markham replied, filling Gabe's glass. "This'll be the last one, pal. As happy as you know I am to take your money, I do have a conscience."

"That'll be the day!" Gabe slurred, downing his glass in one gulp. He rose and wove his way to the door, where his coat and cap hung on the familiar hook. Gabe was a regular.

Outside, his old beagle, Trotty, was barking and racing around in a happy frenzy. Trotty went everywhere with his master and never needed to be tied up. He would wait patiently for Gabe 'til the sun turned into the moon.

"Come on, boy," Gabe said, patting the dog. "We've got a long walk ahead of us. That isn't a bad thing, because at the end of it I should be well sobered up, and then your mistress can't say a word!"

Trotty barked in assent, and together they set off down the dark country road.

It was an unusually quiet night, with hardly any animal noises and no wind. Gabe felt the warm glow of inebriation spread through him, and he whistled a cheery tune. But Trotty wasn't so carefree. When they were about halfway home, he suddenly began to whine.

"What is it, Trot?" Gabe looked down at the dog in surprise.

Trotty was shaking and cowering, his tail between his legs, as if he sensed danger.

The next minute, a terrifying scream tore through the stillness. Gabe no longer needed the long walk home to clear his head; that scream had sobered him up like magic.

In the distance, he thought he could see a figure walking slowly through the gloom. As the figure drew closer, Gabe noticed it was a woman wearing a cloak and a large bonnet. Gabe began walking toward her, but Trotty hung back, whining and whimpering.

"Was it you who screamed?" he asked, when he came up to her.

The woman muttered something that Gabe couldn't make out. Her head was down and completely concealed by the bonnet. Gabe saw that she was carrying a large, cloth-covered market basket.

"Are you all right?" Gabe pressed her. "Can I help you?"

The bonnet shook from side to side. Was she frightened? Or just shy?

Meanwhile, Trotty was tugging at Gabe's sleeve, trying to pull him away. His whines had reached urgent proportions.

"Let go, boy!" Gabe extricated his sleeve from the beagle's mouth.

"He won't hurt you," he assured the woman. "He's really a lamb. But here now. Why would a woman be traveling alone on a dark, lonely night like this?"

The woman did not reply. Instead, she continued on her journey, as if she hadn't heard him. Gabe walked with her.

"Let me at least carry your basket," he offered.

The woman handed him the basket. "Thank you kindly," she replied. Then she laughed. It was not a pleasant laugh. In fact, Gabe would have termed it mocking. Then he realized, with increasing bewilderment, that neither the voice nor the laugh seemed to be coming from his companion.

He tried to look at her more closely, but she averted her gaze. She laughed again—this time a derisive cackle that definitely couldn't have come out of her. It was too close, too loud. Then, to his horror, Gabe realized that the disturbing laughter was coming from the basket he was carrying!

With a yell, he flung the basket onto the ground. It bounced and fell over, and something rolled out. It was a woman's head!

Gabe was too petrified to scream. He stood rooted to the ground, sweat pouring down his face, his breath strangling in his throat.

The woman faced him now. Her shoulders were shaking with the laughter that was coming from the head on the ground. Her bonnet was thrown back—and she had no head!

Now Gabe managed a bloodcurdling scream of his own. And he took off down the road, running for his life.

"Here!" cackled the evil voice behind him. "Take this in payment for your kindness!"

Gabe turned to see the headless horror holding the head in her hand. Then, shrieking with laughter, she flung the thing straight at him.

She should have been a football player, he thought, for she heaved the horrible object with such force that it struck the earth at his feet and bounced around him. And then, Gabe screamed again, for the head was alive! Its eyes glittered maniacally, and its teeth were snapping like a mad dog's. The head rolled toward him, nearly tripping him.

He called for Trotty, but there was no response. In fact, he realized he hadn't seen his dog for quite a few minutes.

Feeling as though he were losing his mind, he looked around for some escape. When he saw a small stream, he suddenly remembered something he'd heard as a child: *A ghost cannot cross moving water.* A superstition, an old wives' tale, whatever it was, it rang in his ears and his heart.

He jumped into the stream, crossed to the other side, and didn't stop running until he reached the top of a hill. Looking down, he saw the ghoul standing on the other side of the stream. The head was rolling about on the ground, screaming and cursing with rage at having been tricked by its victim.

Gabe Fisher ran all the way home, never once looking back. He might be turned into a pillar of salt if he did.

Soaking wet, gasping and trembling, he was met at the door by his irate wife. Trotty stood hiding behind her, whimpering.

"You're not going to believe what I'm about to tell you," he babbled and launched into his incredible story.

"You're right," his wife sneered. "Now, if you told me you were drinking yourself under the table with your cronies at the White Bull, I'd believe you. But getting waylaid by a headless ghost and attacked by a head in a basket? That's your best one yet!"

Later, Gabe told the tale to his neighbors. But his reputation being what it was, nobody believed him. "Better lay off the sauce!" they advised him, snickering.

Nonetheless, it was too good a story to throw away. So the legend of Gabe Fisher and the Headless Ghost became part of the local folklore. As funny as it was, no one who heard it was ever known to take a stroll down that infamous stretch of road, either in darkness or daylight.

As for Gabe, he learned a valuable lesson: When it comes to ghosts, obey your dog!

Chapter 19
The Ghosts
of Ballybrig

In Galway, Ireland, Ballybrig Castle was once home to an intimidating ghostly creature, half man, half…what? It was tall and gangly, with a large pumpkin head and root-like limbs, and was usually sighted in the mist and the darkness, loping about in mysterious, sinister fashion. All who encountered the entity were naturally unnerved by it, but a little dog named Pickle was particularly sensitive to its presence.

The Irish ghost hunter Elliott O'Donnell (1872–1965) was as personally acquainted with phantoms as you and I are with living beings. From the age of five, when he saw his first ghost, "an elemental covered with spots," to his death at age ninety-three, O'Donnell maintained a regular connection to the spirit world and became an internationally known authority on the paranormal.

Some of his claims were, admittedly, a bit on the wild side. O'Donnell said, for example, that a dastardly specter attempted to strangle him in Dublin. He also boasted of being a descendant of several ancient Irish chieftains, among them Niall of the Nine Hostages, otherwise known as the King Arthur of Irish folklore, as well as the sixteenth-century warrior, Red Hugh.

O'Donnell's unorthodox life was the stuff of novels and movies. At the age of twenty-four, looking for adventure, he went to America and became a policeman during the

Chicago Railway Strike of 1894. He tried his hand at several things when he returned to England, including working as a schoolmaster, serving his country in World War I, and acting.

But his true calling was writing. After writing his first book, *For Satan's Sake* (1904), a psychic thriller, and a few more novels, O'Donnell began documenting what he alleged were true accounts of ghosts and hauntings. Altogether, he published more than fifty books and countless articles and essays on supernatural topics. O'Donnell became so famous that he was consulted in numerous paranormal investigations. In later years, he was also a popular radio and television personality.

All in all, it's difficult to discount many of O'Donnell's personal experiences. One in particular—involving a quarry, a ghost, and a dog named Pickle—was truly remarkable.

O'Donnell was visiting his friends, the Dillons, in Ireland. It was his first trip to Galway, and he was looking forward to experiencing this famous part of his native country. The Dillons had recently bought Ballybrig Castle, which was not actually a castle but rather a newly built castellated house. Ballybrig was comfortably isolated, at least a mile from any other property. Among its charms was a beautifully land-scaped terrace lawn and, farther beyond, a rugged field with a hillock and a quarry. High walls enclosed the backyard and a pool, rumored to be fathomless.

As soon as O'Donnell arrived at Ballybrig, he sensed an odd energy.

"I had the feeling that there was something very queer about the house the first night I was in it," he recalled. "Something I had never experienced before, too subtly unusual to explain."

Tired from his long journey, O'Donnell went to bed early that night and promptly fell asleep. Then, he recounted, "something" woke him abruptly.

"I had the feeling something startling was about to happen. The window magnetized me. I got up and went to it. The night was fine and very still; every object in the landscape stood out very clearly. A big, dark Galway hare scurried across the ground, and a night bird hooted dismally."

O'Donnell looked toward the quarry, where he saw a misty shape emerge and advance slowly and purposefully toward the house. It was tall and thin, human in form, but with long, spidery arms and legs and a round head. Loping along in the moonlight, its arms dangling by its sides, it was indeed a creepy sight.

The apparition drew nearer and nearer. Ever the ghost hunter, O'Donnell was far more intrigued than frightened. When the figure moved toward the yard and stables, the house dogs began whining and growling.

The window, said O'Donnell, seemed to hold him in a magnetic grip. Finally, with great effort, he tore himself away from the incredible scene and went back to bed.

The following morning, Nora, one of the Dillon daughters, came down to breakfast looking pale and upset. She'd been awakened, she said, by the dogs barking in the middle of the night, and upon going to the window, she had seen a misty, sinister figure skulking about the grounds. O'Donnell then recounted his experience. There was some interesting conversation at that breakfast table!

The next one to experience the ghost was Pickle the dog.

Nora's sister, Deirdre, was playing fetch with Pickle, the family's Welsh corgi. When Pickle missed the ball, it rolled into a bush. Normally, the little dog would have bounded after it. But as soon as Pickle neared the bush, she stopped short and began to whine and growl, her fur standing on end.

The next thing Deirdre knew, the ball came whizzing out on its own. Pickle barked hysterically and started running, tail between her legs. Deirdre checked the bush, but saw no one. Who, or what, had thrown their ball back to them?

One morning, the third Dillon daughter, Sally, was walking Pickle on the hillock. Suddenly, the dog began whining and pulling on her lead, trying to get Sally to turn back. Sally was astonished, as Pickle had never before acted this way. She was obviously fearful of something. But it was a beautiful morning, and Sally had no intention of returning to the house just yet. So she ignored Pickle's consternation and tried to pull the corgi along. Pickle was as obstinate as could be. She sat down and refused to budge, all the while whining insistently.

Sally was about to give her a swat and a scolding when she suddenly felt something clutch her ankle. She looked down to see a big, bony hand with long, spidery fingers wrapped around it. She screamed, and the hand released her and disappeared into thin air.

Now, Sally was more than willing to take Pickle's advice. She and the dog bolted back to the house. When she related the story to the family, they realized that none of the spooky occurrences could possibly be coincidence or a figment of the imagination. There was a sinister apparition haunting Ballybrig, and why or what its intentions were, they had no idea.

But one of the Dillon boys, Daniel, had a friend by the name of Herbert Ranger, who was a member of the Society for Psychical Research. He phoned Ranger, who obligingly came out to the castle and listened to all the accounts of the ghostly encounters.

Like any thorough researcher, Ranger had to maintain a level of skepticism until the "thing's" existence could be proven beyond a doubt.

"I can't exclude the possibility of it being a case of nerves and imagination with the ladies," he said. "First, Nora thinks she sees a ghost, although it was nighttime and the figure seemed to be coming out of the mist. Could it not be the power of suggestion that caused Deirdre, and then Sally, to have had seemingly supernatural experiences as well?"

"I think not!" Sally snapped. "I saw what I saw. And what about Mr. O'Donnell? He's not crazy. In fact, no one could be more rational. And he saw the ghost."

"He thought he did," Ranger said, shrugging.

No one happened to mention Pickle, the ultimate eyewitness.

"Tell you what," Ranger suggested, "tonight, I'll pay a visit to the quarry, as that's apparently the ghost's hideout."

After supper, everyone sat around talking until the old mantel clock struck eleven. There was an obvious tension in the room, a combination of fear and anticipation, as Ranger rose and put on his overcoat. As he opened the door, Pickle suddenly bolted outside.

"Pickle! Come back, girl!" Deirdre called. But Pickle stubbornly ignored her mistress and stood there, barking up at Ranger.

"I believe she wants to go with you," Daniel said.

"It's almost as if she wants to show you something," O'Donnell remarked.

"I don't know," Ranger was doubtful. "She might disturb the energies. Scare off the entity, you know."

But Pickle was already galloping toward the quarry.

After Ranger left, Sally said, "I hope he sees that ghost, and I hope it scares the pants off of him!"

"Don't hold your breath," Daniel laughed. "I can tell you right now, it takes a hell of a lot to scare Herbert."

"If you ask me, he's just a bit too cocksure," put in Deirdre. "He's bucking for a fall, and our ghost might just give it to him."

An hour later, the front door opened, and Ranger walked into the room, accompanied by a panting Pickle.

"Did you see anything?" everyone cried at once.

"Yes," he said slowly.

"What? Come on, man, tell us!"

Ranger sat down. He looked shaken. "When I got to the quarry, Pickle was already there. She was whining, and her fur was up. As soon as she saw me, she began venturing forward, looking over her shoulder at me all the time, as if to make sure I was following her.

"Then, I saw something. I can't say for sure what it was. A misty figure, part human, part, I should almost say, tree."

"Tree?" Sally giggled. "Now, you've lost me."

"Are you familiar with Professor Tylor, the famed animist?" Ranger asked.

"Of course," O'Donnell answered, while the others shook their heads.

"Well, I imagine it is what he classifies as an elemental. Tylor believes that everything has a spirit, whether animate or inanimate. Trees, rocks, stones—all live harnessed to the things to which they are closely allied until something happens to detach them. In this case, I believe it was the making of the quarry. Somehow, during the disturbance of the rock bed, a nature spirit was let loose and is wandering about."

"Are we in danger?" asked Nora.

"Such spirits can be harmless—or they can be treacherous," Ranger replied. "I don't like to alarm you, but I believe in this case it's the latter. I strongly advise you either to have the quarry filled in or to sell your home."

"Filling in the quarry would be a massive undertaking," said Mr. Dillon.

"Not necessarily," replied Ranger. "First of all, the quarry isn't that deep. Second, the Galway Corporation might be glad to have an additional space to dump their waste. I'll be glad to contact them."

He did, and the quarry was subsequently filled in. That seemed to do the trick.

"When the filling was completed," noted O'Donnell, "the haunting of Ballybrig Castle ceased"—thanks, in part, to a psychic dog named Pickle.

Chapter 20

Dreaming of You

Many of us have had psychic dreams in which we're given infor-mation that is later verified by future events—commonly known as a premonition—or in which we receive a message from some-one who has died, imparting advice, comfort, or a warning. Our passed-on pets, too, come to us in dreams and also can provide solace and guidance, as the following stories prove.

When we dream about our departed pets, we may be simply having a dream—or we may be receiving important mes-sages from them. How can we tell the difference?

Usually, the best way to distinguish between a regular dream and a psychic dream is your gut feeling. When you awaken from a regular dream, you can generally tell that it was just that—only a dream. It may make you feel happy or sad. Often, a wish-fulfillment dream, such as seeing your beloved pet again, can leave you with an acute sense of loss all over again when you awaken and realize that it was only a dream, after all.

A psychic dream—or what I call a "dream that isn't a dream"—is a much more intense experience. Upon awaken-ing, the dream feels as though it were real. You may have the actual sensation of having been with your pet, holding and caressing it. You might still feel the sensation of its tongue on your cheek or its paws on your shoulders. You will tend to feel happy and comforted instead of sad and depressed. Above all, you'll have the unmistakable feeling that your pet was trying to tell you something.

Many years ago, I had a psychic dream about my old cat, Snicky, who died when she was thirteen. Snicky and I had been extraordinarily close from the time I'd rescued her as a tiny kitten. She was all white, which was how she got her name; my then husband was studying Russian at the time, and the Russian word for snow is *snyek*. Bob began calling her "Snyeki," which later became Snicky.

Snicky was a dog-cat. She trailed me everywhere. She slept with me. She fetched things and brought them to me. We played all sorts of games together, some of her own devising, like tag. She'd race over to me and bat me on my leg; then she'd take off. I'd chase her around the house, and she'd dive under something, as if she were yelling, "Safe!" Invariably, though, she was too big to fit in her hiding place. It was hilarious, seeing her big white rear end sticking out from under the bureau or end table, tail waving triumphantly. She was sure she was invisible.

When Bob and I divorced, Snicky was as distressed as any child would have been. I remained in our house, and she grew very dependent on my presence.

One time I went to San Francisco for two months, and my friend Lynn came to house-sit. I figured Snicky would be fine, because Lynn adored her and vice versa. But Lynn became anxious when Snicky refused to eat. She tried all sorts of tempting foods on her, but Snicky would only nibble at the contents of her bowl and then wander off. She seemed depressed and would lie there with the saddest look, as though her world had collapsed around her.

The night I returned, Snicky was beside herself with joy. She circled and circled around me, meowing loudly. When I picked her up, she clung to me. As soon as she was convinced that I was really, truly back, she trotted over to her bowl and began eating ravenously. That should debunk the malicious and totally unfounded myth that cats are aloof, independent, and only come to you for food. Snicky missed me so much that she nearly starved herself. To her, and to most of the cats I've had, love is far more important than mealtime.

✛

The years went by, and I rescued another stray kitten, Angel, and Snicky grudgingly became her big sister. When Angel had kittens, Aunt Snicky endured them. I felt badly that I couldn't give her all of my attention anymore, but she grew to accept her place in our new kitty family.

Eventually, I remarried, and the cats and I moved to my new husband's home, 100 miles away. Amazingly, Snicky, who was now twelve, adjusted once more to a life-altering event. We all lived in happy harmony, until Snicky grew sick and began losing weight. She was constantly throwing up. The vet was unable to diagnose the problem without further and extensive testing.

"She's thirteen years old," he said. "I'll have to put her through a grueling series of stomach X-rays. If we find something, well, frankly I don't know that she'd survive an operation."

We did the X-rays, which, sadly, revealed a tumor in Snicky's intestine.

The vet was completely honest. "Even if she could make it through an operation, I can't guarantee that removing the tumor would cure her," he said. "The cancer has probably spread, given her rapid weight loss. And you certainly don't want to put her through chemotherapy."

I knew he was right, and so I made the agonizing decision to put her to sleep.

I said goodbye to her in her cage at the vet's. She had shrunk to five pounds, and an IV protruded from her thin little leg. I cried my eyes out as I stroked her. She stared at me as though I were betraying her and then turned her head away. I was devastated.

Why I didn't remain with her to the end, I don't know. I've had to put down several cats since then, and I stayed with them while the injection was administered, holding them in my arms until they took their last breath. But Snicky was the first pet I'd ever had to euthanize, and I probably was just too upset to go through the grisly experience of watching her die.

I never forgave myself for that. I couldn't get our last farewell out of my mind. The way she'd turned a cold shoulder to me haunted me for months. I talked to her spirit and begged her to forgive me.

Then, one night about a year after her death, Snicky visited me in a dream that wasn't a dream. I was in a meadow. It was a beautiful, sunny day, and I was walking through thick grass and brilliant wildflowers. Suddenly, I saw a little white cat coming toward me, or rather, the misty figure of a white cat. As she grew closer, she gradually materialized. Realizing that it was Snicky, I shouted for joy.

Snicky ran into my arms. I sank down on the grass, weeping, begging for her forgiveness for my callousness. "I loved you so," I sobbed. "You know I never would have hurt you intentionally. I guess I was just too upset and stupid to understand that you needed me to be there with you until the end."

Snicky cuddled in my arms, purring. She looked up at me, her green-gray eyes full of love. I knew that she was telling me that everything was all right, that she was well and happy, and that all had been forgiven long ago.

It's impossible to describe the joy I felt at having her back. At the same time, I knew she couldn't stay. I held her close until, like the Cheshire Cat in *Alice in Wonderland,* she began to fade away. Her mission accomplished, it was time to go back to the other side.

I awoke at peace. There was no doubt in my mind that Snicky had used the vehicle of a dream to put my heart at rest. She never came to me again in any form, but then, she didn't need to. I knew that everything was all right between us and that she will most certainly be waiting for me when I cross over.

✛

Sometimes, pets appear repeatedly in our dreams to offer even more precise messages of comfort. Such was the case with Joel Davis, whose beloved dog, Archie, passed away of cancer.

Archie was twelve when he developed a malignant tumor. An operation was performed, but the cancer had spread. Like me, Joel had to make the decision all pet owners dread, and like me, he felt a terrible sense of guilt following Archie's death.

"A year passed," he said. "I began to have dreams of Archie. And I kept feeling him around. At times I could almost see him walking beside me as I got up to have my first cup of coffee in the morning. It was like he was still in the house. Yet, something was missing. There was an empty spot inside me that just couldn't be filled."

Joel couldn't imagine getting another dog. How could you replace your best friend? Six months went by, and

Archie began appearing regularly in Joel's' dreams. In one dream, Joel was camping in the woods, and Archie walked up behind him.

"I turned, and there he was with that silly open-mouthed grin he always had. It was then that I saw a white light begin in his chest. The light grew bigger, until it became so bright that I had to shield my eyes. Then the light seemed to fade. When I was able to see again, Archie was not there anymore. In his place was a smaller, black-and-white patched dog, sitting there with Archie's unmistakable grin."

Joel woke up in a cold sweat. Was Archie trying to tell him that he'd reincarnated into this dog? And if so, how was Joel supposed to go about finding him? Should he scour the pet shops or animal shelters, looking for a black-and-white dog with a white patch and a big, silly grin? Or should he wait for a sign that would lead him to the animal?

Joel waited. Six months passed. The black-and-white dog came to him in two more dreams. One day, Joel was on his way to work when, with no warning, he suddenly found himself on the road leading to the city pound. Why or how, he had no idea. The pound was in the opposite direction of his workplace. But he felt that he had to keep going. It was as if an invisible entity had replaced him behind the wheel and was taking him to his destiny.

"I was operating strictly on emotions at this point," he recalled. "I got to the pound and entered the office. This nice woman behind the counter asked if she could help me, and unable to stop myself, I poured out the whole story to her. When I described the black-and-white dog, the woman looked, well, like she had seen a ghost. Her eyes widened, and the color seemed to leave her face.

"'You had better take a look through the door there,' she said.

"So I did. Picture a long row of cages and dogs of all sorts, all barking wildly, vying for attention. But in the first cage to my left was a dog who wasn't making any noise. If it hadn't moved, I wouldn't have even noticed it. When I saw it, it was as if I had suddenly stepped into an ice-cold shower."

It was the black-and-white dog. Every marking was the same as those of the dog Joel had seen in his dream.

The dog was a female, about a year old. She'd been at the pound for some weeks and was scheduled to be euthanized that day. Naturally, Joel adopted her on the spot.

"Jenny has been with me for the last two years now, and the place inside me that was empty isn't empty anymore," he reported. "It's amazing how much like Archie she is. For years I've known that something lives within us and that death is really not the end. But the realization that animals are somehow a part of this and that we are lucky enough to draw their loving spirits to us is truly remarkable. To know a little bit of Archie that I can see and feel lives on in Jenny makes me feel very blessed, indeed."

✛

Fortunately, a pet doesn't have to die to speak to us in dreams. Here, for instance, is the story of a lost cat who sent out a frantic psychic SOS to his young owner in a vivid and disturbing dream.

Eight-year-old Maya and her cat, Crisco, were great buddies. Crisco was a very affectionate young calico who never strayed from home. But one night he disappeared.

Maya was inconsolable. Her parents made numerous visits to the local Humane Society to see whether anyone had reported a lost cat. After a month went by, however, they began to accept the terrible possibility that Crisco was gone forever.

Then one night Maya woke up crying from a bad dream.

"It was awful, Mom," she told her mother. "Crisco was calling me. He said he wants to come home but he can't because he's locked up in a lady's house. He was hiding in a corner and looking out the screen door. The house was messy, and there were dirty dishes all over and junk on the floors."

The next day they received a call from the Humane Society. Someone had phoned about a cat that fit Crisco's description. They gave Maya's mother the phone number. But when she called the number, the woman who answered was surly and hung up on her.

Maya's mother was shocked. Why would this woman call the Humane Society and report a found cat, only to refuse to talk to anyone who contacted her?

Maya's parents had the unshakable feeling that this was their cat. They were determined to get Crisco back, whatever it took. Her father decided to trace the number to an address.

"I can tell you what the house looks like, Daddy," said Maya. She then described the house she had seen in her dream.

Her father finally tracked down the address and drove to the house. Maya's father had no trouble finding the house. It fit Maya's description exactly.

An hour later, he returned home with Crisco sitting happily in the passenger seat. Maya and her mother began to cry.

"I was amazed something like that could happen," said her mother. "Maya's dream is something my husband and I will never forget."

Chapter 21

The Ghost Bear of Boon Hill and Other Apparitions

There are plenty of stories about ghost dogs and cats. But what about other ghost animals? Like bears, for instance? Or pigs, chickens, and monkeys? There's even the ghost goose of Yorkshire, who's said to haunt a churchyard and enjoys spooking horses.

In Staffordshire, England, at the Halmer End Mini Pit, two young workers were on their way to the colliery when they decided to take the shortcut over Boon Hill. It was a chilly January day in 1918, and the men were cold and in a hurry to get to their destination.

As they approached the top of the hill, they got the shock of their lives when a huge bear lumbered out from the trees and started coming after them. Dropping their lunch boxes, the young miners abandoned any notion of going to work and instead ran for their lives, not stopping for breath until they reached Bignal End and home.

Later that day, the residents of Bignal End received word of a terrible mine disaster at the Mini Pit. It was the largest loss of life every recorded in North Staffordshire. Soon, the story spread of the two miners who had escaped the tragedy thanks to a bear on Boon Hill. But no one had ever seen or heard of such an animal. Search parties were formed to look for the bear. They canvassed the local countryside for miles, making inquiries far and wide, but no trace of Ursus Mysterious was ever found.

A local legend could provide the answer . . .

At the end of the twelfth century, Hugh de Audley, the First Earl of Gloucester, left Heighley Castle for a day of hunting. Toward midday, Lord Hugh and his entourage reached Boon Hill. At the summit, he saw a bear in a clearing. He was about to take aim with his bow and arrow when his squire begged him not to shoot, as it was a female bear with her cub in tow. The lord obligingly put away his bow and called off the hunt. The grateful mother bear, it is said, vowed to protect mankind as a man had protected her.

So locals believe that the two young miners who did not make it to Halmer End Mini Pit that fateful day were descendants of the kind Earl of Gloucester and that the bear of Boon Hill—or its ghost—saved their lives that tragic day.

⊹

Another ghost bear is said to haunt the Tower of London.

In 1816, a sentry on guard duty in the former Jewel Tower saw a large bear suddenly appear out of nowhere. Ordinarily, the idea of a bear walking around London would have stretched the imagination to its limits, but in this particular instance, it was plausible; at the time, the Tower had a menagerie containing a variety of animals, including bears.

The bear was so real and so menacing that the terrified sentry assumed it had escaped from its cage, and so he lunged at the animal with his bayonet. But, to his astonishment, the weapon went straight through the bear and hit the wall behind.

The bear vanished before the sentry's eyes, and the poor fellow fainted on the spot. He came to long enough to describe the terrifying encounter, dying several days later from the only apparent cause—shock.

The Jewel Tower menagerie closed in 1835, and the animals were moved to the then newly built London Zoo. But the ghost bear, locals say, continues to prowl the tower—along with the late, beheaded Queen Anne Boleyn and an entourage of other restless spirits who were imprisoned and executed there.

✛

Monkeys, too, can make spectral appearances. One of the more exotic of Britain's animal spirits is the ghost monkey of Athelhampton House in Dorset.

Athelhampton House was originally built by the Martyn family. When we think of a family crest, crowned lions or other lordly beasts come to mind. But the Martyn family crest was admittedly a little weird: a monkey sitting on a tree stump. Over the monkey, on a gilt banner, waved the motto HE WHO LOOKS AT MARTYN'S APE, MARTYN'S APE WILL LOOK AT HIM.

Martyn's monkey was, indeed, real. A family pet who had complete freedom of the house and wandered the halls to his heart's content, unfettered and undisturbed, the primate was actually quite spoiled and doted upon, particularly by one of the Martyn daughters, Alice. The big monkey adored Alice and followed her around like a faithful dog.

But things took a tragic turn when Alice, distraught over an unhappy love affair, decided to commit suicide. She climbed the stairs to a secret room, where she hung herself. Unbeknownst to Alice, the monkey had followed her, undoubtedly sensing his mistress's distress. Alas, he was too late. The monkey, legend has it, began to howl in grief. His near-human cries brought the servants running, and the horrible scene was discovered.

After Alice's death, the monkey refused to eat and slowly starved to death.

Not long afterward, reports began of a ghostly scratching that could be heard coming from the secret room and of the sound of animal feet running on the staircase.

One amazing account came from a guest at Athelhampton, who decided to explore the house. As he was going up the staircase to the secret room, a large monkey suddenly appeared. It was making crying noises. The guest was not frightened, as the primate seemed completely unthreatening. But its appearance was certainly bizarre, as was its departure—the weeping beast slowly faded away, its sobs echoing in the hall after it vanished.

Locals say that Martyn's monkey still haunts Athelhampton House. Chances are, even if you don't seem him, he's surely looking at you.

✛

Another ghost monkey story concerns British spiritualist Harold Sharp, who loved monkeys and kept several as pets. His favorite was a blue mangabey named Mickey.

Mickey was adorable, but he was also a prima donna. He craved attention and would stop at nothing to get it. He was an incorrigible prankster, and one of his antics in particular gained him immortal notoriety in Sharp's village in Leicestershire.

Mickey happened to have an inordinate fondness for candles. He would hold them in his little fingers and chomp on them as one might crunch on carrots. One Sunday morning, Mickey escaped and galloped down the village street and into the church, where the choir was singing. Leaping onto the pulpit, Mickey grabbed a candle and refused to budge until he'd eaten the whole thing, to the indignation of the rector and the delight of the congregation.

Mickey had the very simian habit of searching his fur for saltpeter. "A monkey's perspiration contains a great deal of saltpeter, which crystallizes on the skin," noted Sharp. "They are very fond of eating this, and when bored, they often pass the time away by searching through their fur, seeking these tasty morsels. People who do not understand imagine that they are searching for fleas. If anyone accused Mickey of flea-hunting, he felt it a great indignity and became really angry."

After many years, Mickey passed on to monkey Valhalla. Then, one evening during a session with the medium Jack Webber, Sharp became aware of a pronounced weight on his knee.

"Webber did not know anything about Mickey or my fondness for monkeys," Sharp related. "But he said, 'Do not move, Mr. Sharp, there is a lovely monkey materializing on your knee.' It gradually became visible as Mickey."

Sharp was thrilled, until Webber made a fatal mistake. "No, no, Mickey!" he scolded the monkey. "You must not catch fleas in public!"

"That was enough for Mickey," said Sharp. "With one bound he had gone to where—I hope—no one would misunderstand."

✢

Then there's the phantom horse phenomenon. Ghost horses are quite common, particularly at former battle sites, and may come with or without a ghostly rider.

In the Brandywine Valley of Pennsylvania, numerous witnesses have reported seeing the legendary ghost rider of Chadd's Ford and his famous white steed. The rider is dressed in the traditional officer's uniform of the Revolutionary War and gallops along U.S. Route 1, where the highway intersects with the old Brandywine battlefield. Many a rattled motorist has swerved to avoid hitting the eighteenth-century figure and his beautiful white horse that glows with an unearthly silver light.

The phantom rider is supposedly none other than General "Mad" Anthony Wayne, who, due to a costly strategic blunder made by his commander, George Washington, lost Chadd's Ford during the Battle of Brandywine on September 11, 1777. Apparently, Wayne—an intrepid fighter who hated to lose anything, either bet or battle—never got over the defeat. So, as pigheaded in death as he was in life, he continues to gallop back and forth along the battlefield, spoiling for a second chance.

Another more famous Pennsylvania battlefield boasts more ghosts, both animal and human, than anyplace in the United States: Gettysburg. The area is so haunted that visitors come from all over the world to have a ghost experience, and many aren't disappointed.

One of the famous ghost animals of Gettysburg is the phantom horse of the Wheatfield. The Battle of the Wheatfield was particularly bloody, and visitors to the site regularly report auditory paranormal phenomena—the ghostly sounds of fire crackling, tin cups clinking, and an approaching horse galloping and whinnying.

At Sachs Bridge, spanning Marsh Creek, where Union and Confederate forces advanced during the conflict before the Confederates burned it to cover their retreat, there have been reports of orbs, cold spots, and occasional reenactments of combat by phantom soldiers. But the creepiest ghost is the headless courier, who gallops across the bridge on a black ghost horse—still, they say, trying to deliver his dispatch.

England's battlefields also have their share of phantom steeds—like the famed white horse of Edgehill. The Battle of Edgehill was the first pitched battle of the First English Civil War. A spectral white horse has been seen galloping across the fields along White Horse Road, which runs from the site of the notoriously haunted battlefield to the place where the bodies of the slain soldiers of both armies were buried in 1642.

No one knows for sure who originally owned the white horse of Edgehill. According to one theory, it belonged to Prince Rupert, who survived the battle. Another story names Captain Kingsmill, who died on the battlefield, as the owner. Whoever its master was, the phantom horse is apparently still looking for him.

Not to be outdone, Wales boasts its own ghostly white horse of Colyne Bay. The horse appears in Welsh folklore, but is not confined to legend. It's also been encountered by present-day eyewitnesses, like the man who was driving to work early in the morning. Because his car was unlicensed, he was sticking to the minor back roads.

Just as dawn was breaking, a large white horse appeared from over a hedge. According to the terrified driver, the horse "filled the windscreen." Fully expecting a collision, he braced himself as he slammed on the brakes, his car spinning in the road as it came to a stop. When the driver looked up, the horse had vanished.

Others have seen the Colyne Bay equine apparition, in the same place and at the same time of day, so it can't be attributed to tiredness or hallucinations.

⁜

Then there are ghost animals that annoy horses. One Yorkshire farmer related the following story. He was driving a pony and trap along the road when his horse suddenly shied and bolted. The farmer wrestled with the reins and finally, with great effort, succeeded in getting the animal under control. Mystified as to what had frightened the horse, he looked around and saw what appeared to be a large white goose waddling along the road. When they reached the churchyard, the goose walked right through the large, locked wooden door and vanished.

Upon inquiring, the farmer was told that yes, indeed, he had seen the "ghost goose." The fowl had lived in the churchyard and had the strangest obsession with horses. Whenever it saw one, it began honking and flapping its wings. Then it would lunge at the horse and bite its legs.

The goose died some years back, but its ghost is still a common sight on Melonsby Road, where it apparently continues to get a kick out of spooking the horses!

⁜

One of the weirdest phantom animals has to be the Highgate Chicken Ghost. The story goes that in early April 1626, Sir Francis Bacon, the "father of inductive reasoning," and his friend, Dr. Witherspoon, were driving through Pond Square in a horse-drawn carriage, deep in a discussion about food preservation. The only means of preserving meat in those days was salting, and Bacon was convinced a better method could be found.

It was a bitterly cold day, and Bacon was exploring the possibility of refrigeration. Witherspoon merely laughed at the preposterous notion, prompting Bacon to prove him wrong.

Bacon procured a chicken from one of the surrounding Highgate farms. After killing and cleaning it, he packed it in a large, snow-filled sack and then covered the sack with snow as well.

Unfortunately, Bacon didn't live long enough to find out whether the first frozen chicken was a success. He caught a chill from running around in the snow and died several days later.

Soon afterward, reports began circulating of a plucked chicken that had been observed running in circles around the pond and vanishing into thin air when anyone approached it. The reports have continued down through the centuries. During World War II, air raid wardens often saw the phantom fowl. One warden even tried to capture it, but it vanished through a wall.

In the late 1940s, a visitor to Pond Square heard what sounded like an invisible carriage and horses. As the sound faded away, he saw the naked chicken doing its familiar laps around the pond. He tried to catch it, but as soon as he got close to it, the bird vanished.

The most recent sighting of the Highgate Chicken Ghost was in 1970, when it ran by a couple in the throes of a passionate embrace on a bench by the pond. Talk about a mood killer!

✛

Other barnyard phantoms have also made their way into the paranormal annals. Accounts of pig ghosts include the Isle of Man's "pig of plenty," a white pig that can sometimes be seen on fine, moonlit nights and is believed to bring good fortune to anyone whose path it crosses; the ghost pigs of Merripit Hill, supposedly the apparitions of a sow and her piglets who starved to death hundreds of years ago; and the phantom pig of Berkshire, who, in a case recorded by the Society for Psychical Research in 1908, was seen in the company of a young lady. The case notes read:

> On 2 November, 1907, two young men, Oswald Pittman and Reginald Waud, were painting in the garden of their house, Laburnum Villa. At 10 a.m., Pittman got up to speak to the milkman and saw his friend, Miss Clarissa Miles, coming up the lane. She was due to join the men for a painting session.
>
> Accompanying her like a pet dog was a large white pig with an unusually long snout. When Pittman told Waud about it, Waud asked him to tell Miss Miles to keep the animal outside and close the garden gate securely, as he was a keen gardener and did not want the pig among his plants. However, when Miss Miles arrived, she was alone, and denied all knowledge of the animal. If it had been following her, she pointed out, she would surely have heard it grunting and pattering.
>
> She and Pittman went back up the lane and asked several children if they had seen the pig that

day; none of them had done so. The following morning the milkman, pressed by a bewildered Pittman, signed a statement to the effect that he had not seen a pig, and pointing out that in any case the area was under a swine fever curfew and any stray pig would be destroyed.

Was the phantom pig of Berkshire one of those unfortunate animals? Perhaps. No one has seen it since, but its onetime presence seems to prove that in the animal spirit world, our porcine friends are as welcome as anyone else.

Chapter 22

Cats That Haunt Hotels

Hotels have always been popular haunting grounds for ghost pets. And why not? There's ample food and activity, and there are plenty of rooms to explore. Best of all, there are lots of humans to curl up with. Why cats in particular tend to haunt hotels is a mystery, but there are dozens of reports of hotels with their own ghostly feline residents who have apparently checked in for good.

There is probably no more ghost pet–friendly hotel than the Thayer Historic Bed n' Breakfast in Annandale, Minnesota. Listed on the National Register of Historic Places, the Thayer presents itself as "the Victorian bed and breakfast with personality" . . . and ghost cats.

The Thayer has more ghost cats than you can shake a cat dancer at. That's because new ones always seem to be arriving. Owner Sharon Gammell is no stranger to the paranormal. She's encountered the ghosts of the hotel's former owners many times, along with the ghost of her late husband, Warren, and she hosts regular weekend ghost-hunting tours and classes. So she's perfectly happy to have cat ghosts around as well.

In her book, *Ghost Cats: Human Encounters with Feline Spirits*, Dusty Rainbolt describes the phantom cats at the Thayer. There's GK, short for Ghost Kitty, a playful little gray cat who cavorts and chases things around all day long. GK also likes to stretch out on beds and leaves an indentation in the covers wherever he happens to be snoozing. Guests have actually seen GK in the living room and other public areas; he appears in semisolid form and then dashes off, like any energetic young cat.

GK particularly adores the collection of cat balls owned by Sharon Gammell's current real-life cat, a Maine Coon called Tennessee. She always knows when GK is romping around because she'll hear the toys jingling even when there's nothing near them.

"GK loves to play with these toys," says Sharon.

As for Tennessee, he's not jealous in the least. In fact, he and GK are great pals. Tennessee can often be seen playing tag with an invisible playmate and chasing him around the house.

Kimmie Cat and Clyde Kitty, two other ghost cats at the Thayer, have more serious business to attend to. They are, says Sharon, her "little angels of death," because they always show up when a cat is dying to help him or her cross over to the other side. Sharon recalled the time her beloved cat, Professor Herald, was dying. Kimmie and Clyde appeared like clockwork and stationed themselves on either side of him until he breathed his last breath in Sharon's arms.

Kimmie and Clyde do, however, take time out for fun. Kimmie will often push Gammell's papers off of her desk as a signal for her to take a time-out from work. Clyde is a regular lover boy; if you feel a rough ghostly cat tongue licking you, it's undoubtedly Clyde, who, says Gammell, "gives kisses to people he likes."

Fortunately, Professor Herald is back, too. He's appeared in photos and visits guests. Gammell says there's a surefire way to know if he has climbed into bed with you. If you feel a paw on your shoulder and hear a loud rumbling purr, it's the professor, all right.

Many guests have reported seeing and having tactile encounters with Cocoa Bear, a Maine Coon who died in 1996. If there was the slightest doubt in anyone's mind that Cocoa Bear was around, it was dispelled when the following incident took place.

A four-year-old boy who was at the Thayer with his mother asked if he could play with Gammell's two living cats, Tennessee and Miss Sadie, who were wandering around the parlor. After a while, the child went over to Gammell and asked her how many cats she had.

"Just these two," she replied.

The little boy folded his arms across his chest and looked at her sternly. "No, you don't!" he said. "You have three kitties. Cocoa Bear says he's fine. And how can you miss a big kitty like that? And he's really soft!"

Gammell was dumbfounded. She had never mentioned Cocoa Bear to the little boy. There was no way he could have known about him or that he had been a huge, forty-pound bundle of thick, soft fur.

Another fluffy ghost cat was the newest arrival at the Thayer. Gammell hadn't seen him, but a guest described a gray and white cat. The description matched the dead cat that Gammell found in the yard a week later.

✣

The Crescent Hotel in Eureka Springs, Arkansas, is one of America's most haunted hotels. Built in 1886, it was once a controversial health resort and cancer hospital. Both amateur ghost hunters and professional paranormal investigators have documented the many strange noises and apparitions that have been witnessed there on a regular basis.

Former patients and staff of the hospital are said to haunt the Crescent—like the nurse, dressed in her old-fashioned white uniform, who's still on duty on the third floor, and the "ghost of room 419," who introduces herself to people as a cancer patient and then vanishes.

Numerous guests have seen and heard the "weeping widow," a ghostly woman carrying her young child's blanket and crying in the night. In the lobby, the ghost of a man has been seen hanging out at the bar or standing at the foot of the staircase. A handsome, bearded gentleman in top hat and nineteenth-century dress knocks on doors and inquires, "Are you waiting for me?" There also have been many reports of a not-so-polite spirit who has ripped the covers off of the beds of sleeping guests.

But by far the most appealing of all the apparitions is Morris the cat.

Named because of his resemblance to the famed Morris the cat of the Nine Lives TV commercials, Morris was a big orange tabby who lived at the Crescent Hotel from his birth in 1973 to his death in 1994. He was so beloved by staff and guests alike that he is buried in the hotel's rose garden, his grave marked with a lovely tombstone. He also has a memorial plaque in the hotel lobby, with the following heartfelt tribute:

IN MEMORY OF MORRIS, THE RESIDENT CAT AT THE CRESCENT HOTEL,
HE FILLED HIS POSITION EXCEEDINGLY WELL.
THE GENERAL MANAGER TITLE HE WORE,
WAS PRINTED RIGHT THERE ON HIS OWN OFFICE DOOR.
HE ACTED AS GREETER AND SOMETIMES AS GUIDE,
WHATEVER HIS DUTIES, HE DID THEM WITH PRIDE.
HE CHOSE HIS OWN HOURS AND SET HIS OWN PACE,
THE GUESTS WERE IMPRESSED WITH HIS MANNERS AND GRACE.

UPSTAIRS AND DOWN HE KEPT EVERYTHING NICE,
THEY MIGHT HAVE HAD GHOSTS, BUT THEY NEVER HAD MICE.
DUE TO THE FACT HE WAS GROWING QUITE OLD,
HE'D DOZE BY THE FIRE WHEN THE WEATHER GOT COLD
HIS YEARS WERE A DIGNIFIED TWENTY AND ONE,
WHEN AT LAST HE RETIRED HIS NINE LIVES WERE DONE
HE FILLED HIS POSITION EXCEEDINGLY WELL,
THE RESIDENT CAT AT THE CRESCENT HOTEL.

Morris enjoyed greeting guests from his favorite chair in the lobby and was a most congenial cat concierge. Visitors say that he still sits in his favorite chair from time to time and that he has also been seen wandering around the rose garden. Morris the ghost cat also has been sighted in the hotel's halls, and late at night, guests have called down to the front desk to complain that the sound of a cat meowing in the hall is keeping them awake. A paranormal investigating team even captured Morris's mewing on tape.

✠

The historic Island Hotel in Cedar Key, Florida, is reportedly home to at least thirteen ghosts, one of which is a cat.

The hotel has a long and fascinating history. The structure itself, which dates from 1859, was originally a post office and general store. It was one of the few buildings spared during the Civil War, when Union soldiers burned down most of Cedar Key's buildings—instead, the troops usurped the building as their headquarters. It later functioned as a restaurant and boardinghouse.

In 1914, the building became the Bay Hotel. During Prohibition, it functioned as a speakeasy and brothel. World

War II took its toll on the building, which was quite run-down when Bessie and Loyal Gibbs purchased it in 1946. They renamed it the Island Hotel, and it became a famous watering hole about town. Pearl Buck, Richard Boone, Myrna Loy, and Tennessee Ernie Ford were just a few of the nota-bles who enjoyed the hotel's Southern hospitality.

The most famous part of the hotel is the Neptune Lounge, a small bar that was added in 1946 and features a large painting of King Neptune and his court.

The Island Hotel is seriously haunted. Guests have seen numerous apparitions. The ghost of a little black boy who died before the Civil War and whose skeletal remains were found in the basement has been seen hiding in that area. A Confederate soldier stands guard on the second floor; every morning just as the sun begins to rise, guests can see what appears to be a soldier in a Southern Army uniform standing at attention just inside the doors leading to the balcony. The vision lasts only a few seconds, but has been witnessed by dozens of guests over the years.

The ghost of former owner Simon Feinberg, who was poi-soned by the hotel manager in the 1920s, has been seen wandering the halls at night, startling guests and staff before disappearing.

The most popular and benevolent ghost is Bessie Gibbs, who passed away in 1973, and who apparently continues to watch over the premises. Bessie is said to move around the hotel rearranging furniture and pictures and closing doors. Playful and full of jokes in life, it seems her favorite ghost trick is to lock guests out of their rooms when they step out for a moment. Guests also have seen a ghostly apparition walk through their room and through the walls in the middle of the night. They always describe a spirit resembling Bessie Gibbs.

Bessie loved cats. So it's no wonder that a woman named Cissy had a ghost cat experience at the Island Hotel that she'll never forget.

"This unique hotel has a lot of character, but I didn't notice anything scary about it," she remembered. "The rooms are very peaceful looking, with high four-poster beds. My husband Mike and I were there on a most beautiful day, and the first thing I noticed when we went upstairs was how peaceful it felt."

Cissy was walking ahead of Mike to the balcony when she heard him stop dead in his tracks.

"What is it, honey?" She turned to him.

"Did you see the Siamese cat?" he asked.

"He was pale and really taken aback," Cissy recalled. She couldn't figure out what could be so upsetting about seeing a cat, until Mike described it in detail. He said the cat wasn't "completely there."

"It was some sort of apparition," he insisted.

Because he was so unnerved, Cissy believed him. She wasn't frightened because she loves cats, and figured, *What harm would a ghost cat do, anyway?* But Mike wasn't a cat lover, and it was unusual for him to be so detailed in his description.

That night, they asked the owner if there were any spirit kitties in the hotel. He said if there were, he wasn't aware of them. The next morning, however, when they were talking to the hotel staff about their experience, one of the desk clerks found the story quite interesting. She had been with the hotel since the time of Bessie Gibbs. When Bessie retired, she sold the Island Hotel with the stipulation that the new owners continue feeding all the feral cats who lived outside the hotel—even after her death.

Strangely, Cissy and Mike didn't see any cats walking around the hotel. But the desk clerk and the rest of the staff were convinced that the phantom Siamese was one of the cats Bessie loved. They suspected that the two had reunited and were enjoying the Island's hospitality and maybe even making a little mischief together.

That evening, Mike wanted to turn in early. But Cissy decided to visit the famous Neptune Lounge. While talking to the bartender, she asked him if he'd ever seen a ghost in the hotel.

"Who hasn't?" he laughed.

"How about a ghost cat?"

"Oh, you mean Zsa Zsa?"

"Is she a Siamese?" Cissy asked.

The bartender nodded. "She comes by now and again," he shrugged.

Returning to her room, Cissy was more excited than scared by the verification of the ghost cat. Mike was asleep when she crawled into bed. Feeling "strangely calm and peaceful," she fell into a deep sleep. A few hours later, she was suddenly awakened by a loud bang.

"It sounded like a book had been slammed to the floor. My husband was still asleep, but I woke him up and asked him to check and see if the bible that was on the table next to the bed was still there. It was. Mike got up and turned on the lights, and we both discovered that the phone book that was on a coffee table had been thrown across the room.

"There were supposedly a lot of ghosts in this place, so I'm glad only one benevolent trick was pulled on me. I still think it's funny that my husband, who hates cats and doesn't believe in ghosts, should have been the one to see a ghost cat!"

Chapter 23

Pepper's Ghost

When negative entities haunt a dwelling, it's often our animals who sense them and try to make us aware of them. As we've seen in many stories in this book, our pets can alert us to danger before we sense it ourselves. When it comes to dangerous ghosts, they will often urge us, in strident animal language, to follow their lead for a change.

Pepper was Kristy's angel girl. A beautiful, bouncy Australian shepherd, Pepper was an unusually happy dog who always managed to lighten things up, and when her mistress got in a funk, she would remind her to chill out with a laugh.

But when Kristy and her husband moved to a new house, Pepper began to act strangely. While in the past she'd always followed Kristy everywhere and obeyed her commands, now she refused to come inside and would cower at the door, whimpering. Kristy had to drag her in by the collar, not an easy task for the diminutive woman, as Pepper was a stubborn sixty pounds.

Pepper also developed insomnia and anxiety. She would pace and pace at night, standing next to Kristy's bed and panting loudly. Kristy told herself it was just a phase and that Pepper would soon acclimate to her new home. But when several more weeks went by with no improvement in Pepper's disposition, Kristy took the distressed dog to the vet for a thorough checkup.

Pepper tested perfectly fine and healthy, at least physically. The vet prescribed a mild antianxiety medication, which Kristy wasn't thrilled about, as she knew it would only mask the problem. But since there seemed to be no alternative, she followed the doctor's orders. No one in the house was getting any sleep, and perhaps the pills would calm Pepper down and give them all a decent night's rest.

After two weeks, however, there was no improvement in Pepper's condition. The drugs only made her sleepy. She was still anxious and distressed.

The vet prescribed a stronger medication, to no avail. Meanwhile, Pepper seemed to grow worse. She took to hiding under the bed for long periods. In the living room, she would huddle in the corner.

One of the most inexplicable shifts in her behavior concerned a dark brown recliner. Until the move, this had been Pepper's favorite piece of furniture. She was always curling up in it, to sleep or to watch TV with Kristy and her husband, who groused good-naturedly about how Pepper had usurped his throne. But now, Pepper acted as though the chair were an enemy. She would growl at it and back away from it. When anyone approached it, she would whine loudly, as if trying to dissuade them from sitting in it.

Kristy's friend knew of a pet psychic in the area. Ordinarily, Kristy would have pooh-poohed the idea of animal mind reading, but she was desperate enough to try anything. She made an appointment with the psychic, and they met the next day in the woman's office.

The psychic instantly connected with Pepper. She described the dog exactly and said that there was a spirit in Kristy's house that only Pepper could see. Pepper was upset because she knew the entity wasn't supposed to be there. As the dog put it, "He's a grumpy old man who wants to leave, but he can't."

Kristy didn't know what to think. It all sounded too crazy to believe. Pepper talking? Just like a person?

"Is she actually speaking to you?" she asked the psychic.

"No, it's more [like] she's sending me pictures," the woman replied. "And I'm sensing Pepper's emotions. She is extremely anxious; this spirit is bothering her [to] no end."

Then the psychic began describing Kristy's house in great detail. Kristy was astounded—even more so when the psychic said, "You have a dark-colored chair in the living room, don't you?"

"Yes," Kristy said. "A brown recliner."

"Well, this spirit likes to sit in that chair. And it upsets Pepper."

Kristy thought of how the chair used to be Pepper's favorite spot and how, after they'd moved, she'd done a 180-degree turn and refused to go near it.

She then asked the psychic what Pepper's favorite toy was. After a few seconds, the psychic replied, "The bear."

Pepper had many toys, but her favorite was a little stuffed bear that she dragged everywhere with her.

Kristy asked the psychic if she could do anything to calm Pepper down.

"The spirit needs to leave, for its sake and yours," the psychic replied. "Go home and burn sage leaves throughout the house, concentrating on the room with the chair. This is what we call 'smudging.' It's an ancient and powerful purification ritual. Then, command the spirit to leave and never return. Tell it to look for the light, wish it well, and give it the boot!"

On the way home, Kristy stopped at the local herbalist shop and bought a pound of sage leaves. That night, she and her husband followed the psychic's instructions, smudging the house and giving the spirit its walking papers. They repeated the ritual for three more days. Miraculously, on the fourth day of smudging, Pepper was back to her old self. She begged to come inside and reclaimed her old chair. She was happy and playful again. It was as though nothing had ever happened.

Kristy is thrilled to have Pepper back and the house ghost-free. But she says she's keeping a supply of sage leaves on hand, just in case!

⁜

A similar story involved a dog, a cat, and a haunted staircase.

"I have one staircase in my house," wrote Valerie Miller in a post to www.globalpsychics.com. "My cat has severe sei zures whenever she comes down the stairs. Finally, when we confined her out of reach of the stairs, the seizures stopped, and she has been fine for the last year and a half.

"But my dog, a large black Lab, has had a few incidents in the vicinity of the staircase. One was very traumatic. He was terrified of something on the ceiling near the staircase. And now, a year later, he still refuses to go down the stairs. I have to drag him, yipping the whole way. He seems like he's in pain. Once down, he's okay and bounds off. Here's the strangest part: he has no trouble going up the stairs, only down."

Valerie was advised to research the history of the house and the area and to contact a psychic in order to initiate a clearing of the premises. She discovered a dark secret from the house's past: In the 1930s, the owner of the house mur-dered his wife by pushing her down the staircase. Valerie immediately got a referral to a psychic, who came to the house and did a clearing ritual, which had to be repeated several times before the unhappy entity finally departed. They knew the spirit was gone when Valerie's Labrador began descending the staircase with no apparent distress.

⟡

According to the Spiritual Science Research Foundation, "All animals can perceive the negative vibrations emanating from ghosts, but they cannot identify the details, such as what is the type of ghost, its strength, its motive, what to do to defend oneself, etc. Dogs, horses, crows, and cats are better known for their ability to perceive the presence of ghosts."

One such four-footed clairvoyant was Chanel, a black-and-white stray who had been adopted by a family when she was still a kitten. The family lived in an old attached house that had never shown any indication of being haunted. But from the moment she arrived at her new home, Chanel was spooked.

"She would look at the stairs, her gaze slowly moving from the bottom to the top, as if she was observing someone walking up the steps," said her owner, Jeanne M. "At other times, her green eyes would be transfixed upon a certain spot on the ceiling above me. While I couldn't see anything, Chanel was definitely watching something."

One evening, Jeanne was sitting in the living room with Chanel on her lap. As usual, the cat was fixated on the ceiling but seemed to be even more excited than usual. Suddenly, the ceiling began to shake with heavy, thumping steps. It sounded, said Jeanne, like a big man with extremely heavy boots was walking on the living room ceiling *upside down*!

Jeanne was terrified, and Chanel was absolutely frantic. She stared at the ceiling, hissing and spitting until the deafening racket stopped. Immediately, Chanel turned away from the ceiling and settled down. Jeanne checked the upstairs rooms, but there was no one else in the house.

The heavy-footed entity never returned. But Jeanne was amazed at how Chanel was able to sense something, or someone, on the ceiling long before the incident occurred.

⊹

Geoffrey, a seeing eye–trained German shepherd, and his brother, Rufus, a large golden retriever, could certainly see ghosts. They were the first to notice an unsettled, and unsettling, entity in the Prescott house.

Denise Prescott, then fifteen, was alone in the house one afternoon watching TV, when Geoffrey, who was lying contentedly at her feet, suddenly began to growl. At the same time, Rufus ran and hid behind a large plant in the corner. Denise had to laugh at the ridiculous sight of the big dog cowering behind the plant as though it could possibly conceal him.

But it was no laughing matter when a gust of cold air brushed past Denise and Geoffrey jumped up and started snarling. When Denise saw that the hair on the back of the dog's neck was standing up, she got goose bumps. Geoffrey moved to the top of the stairs that led into the basement family room, and he continued to growl and snarl as he looked down into the dark basement.

Terrified that someone had broken into the house, Denise turned on the downstairs light and went down the steps with Geoffrey in front of her as a canine shield. But there was nothing in the basement. Nonetheless, Geoffrey continued to growl. At that moment, Denise heard the plaintive sobs of a little girl. Geoffrey backed up, as if someone were approaching him, and his growls became louder and more threatening.

Denise bolted up the stairs. Meanwhile, Rufus was still cowering behind the plant, whining and sniffing at the vent in the living room floor. Through the vent, Denise could hear the faint ghostly sobs, coming up from the basement. Terrified, she called her boyfriend and begged him to come over and stay with her until her parents came home.

When her parents heard the story, they decided to do some investigating. Inquiring about the house's history, they learned that a child named Mary had died there during the terrible influenza epidemic of 1918. Although the young girl's spirit could hardly be termed menacing, both Geoffrey and Rufus were obviously disturbed by it. Undoubtedly, like Pepper, they sensed that the ghost was unhappy, and its negative energy was adversely affecting them.

$$\cdot\hspace{-0.2em}\dagger\hspace{-0.2em}\cdot$$

While Mary was only a mildly disturbing spooky presence on occasion, other ghosts can wreak true havoc, dismantling people's lives. For its TV series *The Haunted,* Animal Planet investigated the story of Tom and Deborah Weaver, a Cleveland, Ohio, family beset by ghosts who tormented both them and their dogs, Trouble and Georgia.

"It seemed to start with one spirit and then progressed to the point where we identified seven of them," said Deborah. "Our dogs were the first to notice that something strange was going on in our living room."

Trouble began barking and chasing something the

Weavers couldn't see. Often, she would sit staring into space and pawing at the air. Trouble became so distraught that the Weavers took her to the vet, but there was no physical explanation for her behavior.

A few weeks later, the Weavers began experiencing ghostly phenomena in the living room and hallway. Soon, the spirits were acting up on a daily basis. The couple heard weird noises and felt disembodied presences. Objects either were moved by something or someone or moved by themselves. Trouble and Georgia were constantly freaked out. Finally, at their wit's end, Tom and Deborah told a few family members about their ordeal and asked them over to see if they, too, could sense the strange goings on.

One—Deborah's sister, Laura Templin—was an inveterate skeptic. But when she felt "something" touch her on the neck and shoulder, she became a believer on the spot.

"Oh, my goodness, I jumped up and ran out of the house!" Templin later told reporters.

Chris Page, who runs the "Orbs" paranormal detection agency featured in *The Haunted,* admitted to witnessing supernatural phenomena at the Weavers' residence. "There is no doubt that something extraordinary is going on in this home," said Page. "This goes way beyond just the data showing up on our meters. I have no doubt there is paranormal activity going on here."

✥

Finally, there's my own story.

In my book, *Haunted Christmas,* I related the story of my brief but wonderful marriage to my late husband, Adam Shields, and the psychic I met by chance on Christmas Eve, four months after his death, who gave me distinct messages from him and brought me the comfort I needed to get through the most difficult holiday season of my life. But there is more to that story.

Although Adam was twenty-three years older than I, we had so much in common that I never felt the age difference. We had the same crazy sense of humor. We shared a love of history, film, literature, art, and music. We were homebodies who just loved being together.

And we adored cats. We had four of our own cats and an entire entourage of strays who would show up at our door at mealtime. One of our favorite outings was going to the local pet store to get, as Adam put it, a "kitten fix."

"I say, love," he'd suggest in his lilting Dublin accent, "why don't we go down to Pet Headquarters and pick up a six-pack of kittens?"

Of course, he was just kidding about the six-pack. Neither of us had any intention of adding to our feline collection. We just enjoyed visiting the kittens and watching their antics. Free entertainment!

Adam was a staunch cat person. He was not fond of dogs and classified them into two categories: "woofers" and "tweeters." I, on the other hand, loved all animals, and although I'd never had a dog, I toyed with the idea of getting a Chihuahua.

"Absolutely not!" Adam would reply whenever I pestered him about it. "I'll have no tweeters in this house!"

But when he was dying of lung cancer, he told our home aide, "I know that when I die, Mary Beth is going to get a Chihuahua."

I felt terrible. What did he think, that I was waiting for him to expire so that I could run out and get a tweeter?

Adam was the love of my life, and I had no idea how I was going to live without him. He died in August of 1996, and as Christmas approached, my grief intensified. One dismal December day, I decided to cheer myself up with a kitten fix. I went to Pet Headquarters, but they were out of kittens. However, they did have a three-pound black and tan Chihuahua puppy.

I went over to the glass-enclosed puppy playpen. The little fellow looked at me intently, one ear up and one ear down. He was the cutest thing I'd ever seen. When the store clerk uttered the fatal words, "Want to hold him?" it was basically all over. I cuddled the puppy under my chin, and he licked my face ecstatically. I considered taking him home then and there.

Reason, however, prevailed. First of all, I was in the process of selling the house and moving back to Los Angeles, where all of my friends were. I was in no position to take on a puppy, an undertaking as demanding as having a child. Second, there were the cats to consider. They, too, were deeply affected by Adam's death, and introducing a new pet—let alone a dog—into the household would be one more trauma. Third, the puppy, being pedigreed, cost $600. That came to $200 a pound. I'd have to be out of my mind.

I handed the puppy back to the store clerk, congratulating myself on my fortitude and good sense. But on Christmas Eve when I went to Barnes & Noble to get a book for my brother, I ran into a young woman who asked me, out of the blue, "Have you lost someone recently?"

"Yes," I said. "My husband."

This girl, whose name was Andrea, proceeded to describe Adam to me in chillingly accurate detail.

"I'm psychic, you know," she said matter-of-factly. "And I think I'm getting a message from your husband."

She relayed several messages that involved information she could not have known. I was flabbergasted. Then she said, "Do you have a little dog?"

"No," I replied.

"But you're thinking of getting one, aren't you?"

I nodded.

"Your husband wants you to get that dog."

Adam giving me the go-ahead to get a tweeter? Right!

But I couldn't get the puppy out of my mind. Finally, on New Year's Eve day, I went back to Pet Headquarters, fully expecting to find him gone. But he was still there. I plunked down $600, plus another $200 for everything from sweaters to squeaky toys, wee-wee pads, and all sorts of other essential puppy paraphernalia. I named him Truman, after my favorite president, Harry Truman. Then I took him home to three hostile cats.

Truman survived that introduction and has been with me fifteen years now. My dearest, most faithful companion, he brought me through the darkest period of my life and taught me how to live and laugh again.

I've always felt that Adam guided me to Truman. So it makes perfect sense that Truman would be able to see his ghost.

A year after Adam's death, I sold the house and returned to Los Angeles, where I found an adorable little house to rent. Several nights after I moved in, I was busy unpacking when Truman, who was now ten months old, suddenly began growling and baring his teeth.

It was around 1:00 a.m. on a balmy July night. A soft breeze and the heady scent of night-blooming jasmine floated in through the open windows. All was calm and still—except for Truman.

Now, I have had quite a few encounters with the paranormal, but I am not a clairvoyant. I'm what you call *clairaudient,* or *clairsentient;* I can sense spirits, feel them, and on occasion receive psychic messages from them. But I've never actually seen a ghost.

Truman, however, was definitely seeing something, because in addition to staring and snarling at the naked air, he was backing up as if someone were coming toward him.

"Who is it, Truman?" I asked.

Then, I felt Adam's presence. I could almost see his sweet, kind face and hear his soft, gentle laugh. A feeling of love and joy washed over me. My beloved husband was really with me, looking out for me, making sure I was all right as I picked up the pieces and went on with my life.

And here was a little tweeter, yipping and yapping at him!

"Honey," I said, "you told me to get him. And now you'll have to put up with him."

I turned to Truman. "He's really a very nice man," I said. "I know he says he doesn't like tweeters, but give him time. He'll warm up to you."

Truman looked up at me and snorted—one of those weird Chihuahua snorts that sounds like a grunt, a cough, and a sneeze all rolled into one. He stopped snarling, but he still continued to stare at what I presumed to be Adam, as if he were sizing him up.

Fourteen years have passed since that memorable night. Truman is now old and gray and rotund with age. We have journeyed far and wide together and lived in many places. But sometimes late at night lying fast asleep on my bed, he'll awaken with a start and stare into the darkness, growling softly at an invisible someone who's no longer a threat.

I suspect that Adam has finally warmed up to him.

Chapter 24
Possessed

One of the oldest questions pondered by mankind is this: Can animals be demonically possessed? Debates have raged for centuries on this issue. Some religions and cultures believe that demons can possess anything, from people to plants, animals, insects, rocks . . . you name it, they haunt it. Others maintain that it is necessary to have a soul in order to be possessed and that it has yet to be proven whether animals have souls.

Well, we animal lovers know that animals do have souls. And there are a number of cases of dogs, cats, and other pets acting so weirdly and maniacally that demonic possession seems like the only logical explanation for their bizarre behavior.

Could a pet that was once your most loving companion suddenly become demonically possessed?

Jarrod would say, absolutely.

When he was eight, Jarrod woke up one morning to what would turn out to be the strangest day of his childhood. It began with an overpowering feeling of suffocation, as if, he would later recall, a huge crowd was bearing down on him. He also felt an extraordinary clarity, as though "a veil had been uncovered from within."

Nothing particularly strange happened that day at school. But afterward as he was walking home, Jarrod began experiencing odd, inexplicable phenomena, like seeing a dog only through his right eye and having people he'd never seen before appearing in shadow and disappearing. It all seemed like a new world to him, as though he'd been somehow transported to another dimension.

Jarrod was too bewildered to talk about his strange experiences to anyone. Instead, he tried to put them out of his mind by turning to his usual after-school activities: eating a snack and playing with his younger brother, Kevin.

All seemed back to normal as Jarrod and Kevin drew cartoons in the dining room while their parents watched TV. Suddenly, both boys heard the sound of scurrying paws and clacking nails on the floor near the kitchen. They figured it was probably the family cat and dog, Dusty and Roddy, playing their favorite game of tag. But when Jarrod went to check it out, he found no animals around.

Roddy, it turned out, was in the backyard chasing squirrels. The boys began calling for Dusty. As if in response, the dining room table suddenly jumped and moved several feet. A minute later, their father shouted from the living room that Dusty was in his lap.

Jarrod and Kevin panicked. What was in the kitchen? They ran to their parents and told them about the strange animal noises and the levitating table. Their mother went into the dining room and kitchen to investigate but found nothing out of the ordinary.

Jarrod, however, had begun to glimpse a dark, smoky form out of the corner of his eye. It wasn't a shadow, he knew, because it was denser and more mobile than a shadow would be in mid-afternoon. But when he turned to look, the form was gone.

After dinner, the family sat down to watch TV. Dusty was in Jarrod's lap, purring. But Jarrod also heard purrs and meowing that were definitely not coming from his cat. The sounds seemed to be coming from behind him. He became really frightened when they began to change to hisses and yowls. Yet, when he cried out, everyone else in the room turned and stared at him. They hadn't heard a thing.

In bed that night, Jarrod felt cramped, as though "I was supposed to make room for someone." He scooted to the far side of the bed against the wall. For a long time he lay awake, mystified and frightened by the day's strange events. Then, just as he was dozing off, he heard purring. Knowing that Dusty was underneath the bed, he tried to ignore her, but there was something unusual about the sound. It was quite loud, louder than Dusty's normal purr.

Then Jarrod froze as the purring changed to the sound of gargling and snarling, "as if my cat had been choked and force-fed something at the same time." Suddenly, he felt Dusty jump on the bed. Sitting up, he found himself staring into a pair of glaring yellow eyes. Then, to his horror, Dusty bared her fangs, hissing and snarling at the little boy.

This was completely freakish. Dusty was, said Jarrod, "my dearest friend in the world." What happened next was truly horrifying. Claws out, Dusty viciously attacked Jarrod, who screamed and covered himself with his pillow. But this didn't stop the crazed cat, who slashed and tore at the pillow, trying to get at him.

Awakened by the noise, Jarrod's father rushed into the room. As soon as he switched on the lights, the madness stopped, and Dusty suddenly collapsed in a limp heap. She was dead.

As she lay there, Jarrod saw what seemed like a dark mist seeping out of her fur. The mist hovered over her body before fading away.

To this day, Jarrod bears the scars from where Dusty's claws slashed his arm. There is no doubt in his mind that his beloved cat had suffered a fatal attack of demonic possession.

✠

A woman named Sharon had a similarly horrific experience when her basset hound, Georgia, turned on her out of the blue.

"I was reading a book when I heard my dog snarling like there was an intruder," she wrote in an online post. "So I carefully went outside to take a look around."

To Sharon's surprise, Georgia stood there growling at her boyfriend, Brian. This was completely out of character, as the dog loved Brian. Then, turning around, Georgia began to snarl at Sharon.

"I instantly saw that her eyes were devil red. She started to growl and snap at me, and I had no idea what was going on. Nothing like this had ever happened before.

"Suddenly, I saw this white figure appear from behind Georgia and rush into the house. I was so scared I couldn't even scream. Even my boyfriend, who says he's not afraid of anything, was in a quivering heap."

The sound of banging and crashing brought Sharon and Brian running into the kitchen. They stood there, transfixed with horror, as cupboards opened and shut, the refrigerator gurgled, and water gushed from the tap. Meanwhile, Georgia had gone completely berserk and was racing around the house yowling.

Sharon never discovered who the figure was or what had turned Georgia into a devil dog. But Sharon was convinced that this sinister ghostly entity had something to do with the demonic possession of her gentle basset.

✠

Animal Planet's popular ghost-busting series, *The Haunted,* features a number of stories about possessed animals. One, "Demon House," is particularly chilling. It concerns the two-hundred-year-old home of a couple named Jake and Elke, which was, it turned out, a hotbed of evil.

The terror began when Elke heard a sinister voice coming through her baby monitor, saying, "You are all going to die!" It was the beginning of a horrifying demonic siege that spared no one. Soon after the chilling warning, Jake and Elke heard a loud crash in their children's bedroom. When they ran into the room, they were greeted by a ghastly sight: the baby's crib was covered with bloody handprints.

Jay and Elke knew they needed the help of paranormal professionals—and quickly. They contacted Connecticut Paranormal Investigators, who work closely with Catholic priest and veteran demonologist Father Bob Bailey.

During the investigation, Elke's older dog, Mandy, went into convulsions. Knowing a case of possession when he saw it, Father Bob rushed over to the thrashing, drooling animal and immediately began praying over it. As the prayers ended, the dog stopped shaking and returned to normal.

But all was not over. The entity was still around, and it was not a happy camper. Father Bob rolled up his sleeves and prepared for an intense spiritual battle, and priest and demon duked it out, with God emerging the victor.

⊹

It's not only your typical house pet that can become possessed. One woman reported that she and her brother encountered a possessed groundhog "screaming like a child in excruciating pain."

An uncle who was also there ran into the house and returned with his high power rifle. He shot the animal three times in the head, and as it was dying, it was heard to cry out, "Mommy!"

✛

Perhaps you caught the stranger-than-fiction story out of East Sussex, England, about the world's biggest bunny. The story made headlines in 2010.

At the time, Ralph, a continental giant rabbit, weighed forty-two pounds and was two feet long and still growing. At not quite a year old, Ralph weighed more than your average three-year-old child. He devoured around $600 worth of food per month, and his owner, Pauline Grant, relied on the donations of neighbors to meet the daunting grocery bill.

"He has quite the appetite," observed Grant. "It really hits us in the pocket having to feed him, but thankfully, Ralph is so famous in the area people stop me in supermarkets and offer to fit the bill."

Ralph is adorable, but unfortunately he's too big to pick up and cuddle.

"I have no idea how big he is going to get," Grant admitted. "But everyone loves him, and he laps up the attention."

No one so much as considered the possibility that Ralph's gigantism could be the work of the supernatural, until TV medium Derek Acorah, star of the *Most Haunted* series, suggested that possession might be at work.

"We are pretty sure our house is haunted by something or other," Grant admitted.

Acorah met Ralph in London and had "a good old chat" with the amiable bunny about the spirits in Grant's house. The conclusion: Ralph was channeling the spirit of a ghoul.

Grant was skeptical but intrigued. "It sounded like a lot of nonsense," she laughed. "But then again, you have to admit that Ralph is not your average rabbit."

✛

I, too, might be harboring a possessed pet. His name is Lincoln Aurelius, and he's a stray kitten who appeared in my garage one November morning, meowing at the top of his lungs. I scooped him up and kissed him, and his strident mews changed to a loud, happy purr.

I brought him inside and fed him. He devoured two cans of Fancy Feast, after which he went exploring and immediately started getting into mischief. He chewed the TV cable, jumped into the dishwasher and rattled around in the clean dishes, got into the bathroom and unrolled the toilet paper, ate my Chihuahua's food, and killed any stray plastic grocery bags he found. That wasn't unusual, of course, for a four-month-old kitten. But a veritable siege of terror was underway.

Lincoln was a five-pound cyclone. He whizzed through the house destroying everything in his path. He pushed everything off of counters and tables: dishes; glasses, full or empty; pill bottles; plants; the telephone; and basically anything he could get his paws on. The day he pushed my laptop off my desk and nearly destroyed my life's work was a day that shall live in infamy.

Particularly fascinated with water, Lincoln spent a good deal of time peering into the toilet and sitting in the sink batting at the water flowing from the tap. He also loved paper of any kind, and my floor was littered with shredded mail, paper towels, and torn-up tissues. He attacked anything that moved, including feet. He'd grab me by the leg when I was walking by, biting my toes and hanging on to my ankle for dear life with his claws. If I couldn't shake him off, I ended up walking around with a cat ball attached to my ankle.

Lincoln would run laps around the kitchen and living room, whizzing by in a blur, until he collapsed from exhaustion and promptly fell asleep wherever he happened to drop. Or he'd lunge across the room and leap onto the wall, sliding down by his claws. I have had many kittens, but never one as wild as this.

I began to wonder if he was possessed. After all, he looked like a demon. He was all black, from the tip of his ears to his tiny paw pads. When you looked at him from a distance, all you could see were two huge yellow eyes, like searchlights peering out of the darkness. He was long and sleek like a panther, and a snaggletooth poked out of the side of his mouth. If he hadn't been so little and cute, he really would have given me the willies.

"Welcome to kittenhood!" laughed my friends.

But I knew it was a case of more than mere youthful energy when one night Lincoln jumped on my bed and approached me with a strange, intense look in his amber eyes. He crept up my leg, stomach, and chest until his face was in mine. It reminded me of one of my husband's wittier comments, when our cats used to walk on me: "Do you ever feel like the runway at a cat fashion show?"

I was reading and wearing my glasses. The next thing I knew, a little black paw reached out and pulled off my glasses, just as my ten-month-old grand-niece loved to do. Then, to my horror, Lincoln stuck his nose in my eye and bit my eyelid! I yelled and put my hands up to my face. He was purring in some sort of trancelike fit, a deep rumble that grew louder and louder as he batted at my hands and pushed his head against my cheek. I dove under the covers, pulling them tight around me, but he pushed under them somehow and made for my face again. I finally threw him out into the hall and closed the bedroom door. But he proceeded to drive me insane by clawing at the door and meowing piteously.

I kept my bedroom door open because my Chihuahua, Truman, and my other cat, Junior, always slept with me. Unwilling to lock them out, I tried to protect myself from Lincoln, but he was rock-jaw determined to get at my eyes. During the rare moments when he was sleepy and docile, I'd hold him and kiss him, thinking I was safe as he laid there, eyes closed, purring so loudly I almost needed earplugs. But I never knew when, in a flash, the claws would come out and Lincoln would take a swipe at my eye or jump up and try to eat it.

I consulted my vet, who admitted that she had never encountered such behavior in a kitten or cat or any animal, for that matter. I decided that Lincoln was possessed by an eyeball-craving incubus.

Everyone told me to get rid of him. Pronto. But I had no luck finding him a home, and I couldn't bear the thought of a shelter. Besides, he had his irresistible side. He could be so adorable, butting his head against me in gratitude when I fed him or lying against me and holding my hand against his cheek with his soft little paws.

As the weeks passed and I looked tenderly down at his little demon face with the wild yellow eyes and the tiny snaggletooth, I knew I was falling in love. It was sort of like *Rosemary's Baby,* when Rosemary finally discovers that her newborn infant isn't dead, after all, and finds him in the black-draped bassinet during that hilarious satanic open house. At first she's horrified: "His eyes!" she screams. Yellow, we presume. And his little hooves and claws . . . But then she starts to rock him, and pretty soon she's smiling down at him with a mother's love and you know she's hooked.

It's the same with Lincoln. He may be a little demon, but he's *my* little demon.

Chapter 25

The Haunted
Harnesses

If a pet can be haunted, why not his or her accessories? Haunted objects are a common aspect of the paranormal; entities often use objects to get our attention, causing them to move or disappear. According to paranormal researcher Melba Goodwyn, "Ghosts use objects to communicate or deliver messages. In this case, objects may become carriers of psychic content." Psychic Sylvia Brown observes that "a spirit might have a lingering fondness for an object and want to come visit it. Every object is capable of holding an imprint that may or may not be a happy one."

Our final chapter recounts the stories of two dog owners who encountered some spooky activity around their pet's harnesses.

It was a sunny, lazy Kentucky afternoon, and Jenna was in the living room of her small, comfortable apartment playing around with her laptop. To her left was the TV. On her right she could see the front door and the pair of dog harnesses hanging on a hook next to it.

Jenna was looking back and forth from the TV to her laptop when, out of the corner of her eye, she thought she saw one of the harnesses move. Thinking she'd imagined it, she went back to the computer. But at that moment, one of her Chihuahuas, Salsa, who had been asleep on the couch, jumped down and went over to the harness. Standing about three feet away, she stared at the object. Suddenly, the harness began to bounce up and down. Jenna recalled that it was as if "someone was holding the leash and moving it to make the harness dance."

"I had clear vision around the whole harness," she explained, "and what I really saw was just like someone pulling up on it, as if it were a puppet on a string."

Meanwhile Roxy, Jenna's other Chihuahua began barking furiously at the harness and keeping her back to the door. Jenna knew her dogs were seeing something she wasn't, as they only barked at visitors and never at their harnesses or any other object.

Jenna looked at the harness and tried to figure out why or how it was doing its ghostly dance. *There must be a rational explanation,* she told herself. But she could find none. There was no breeze that could have caused the movement, as the living room fan was turned off.

Then, as the bouncing stopped, both little dogs looked slowly up the wall and began barking hysterically at a corner of the ceiling. Jenna was quite frightened and tried to hush the dogs. They quit their barking, but continued to stare up at the ceiling, trembling.

Jenna was scared out of her wits. She never did find out what spirit was haunting the harnesses, but she immediately got rid of them and bought another, completely different set that, so far, seems stationary.

✛

Apparently, haunted harnesses aren't that uncommon. Take the following story.

Alison had two fox terriers: Lexie, who loved to ride in her Lexus, and Bunny, so named because she liked to chase rabbits. Bunny was very active and hated to just sit around. She loved to be out in the sun playing "fetch" or just running around. Because their large yard was not enclosed, Bunny was sometimes tied to a tree with a long cable attached to her leash and harness. The cable gave her ample room to romp.

One day when Alison brought Bunny into the house, she noticed that her harness—a full body harness made of a strong nylon material—had been cut. Upset that someone had gotten into the yard and afraid that whoever it was might have been trying to take the dog, Alison kept close watch over Bunny from then on, keeping her on just a leash and collar. Eventually, she bought Bunny another extremely durable harness that she was confident couldn't be tampered with.

One night when Alison and her roommate had been with their dogs all evening and Bunny had been wearing her harness, Alison let the dog out for a few minutes to do her business. When the girls went to bed, Bunny was still wearing the harness. Alison unsnapped it and placed it on top of her crate, where the dogs slept next to the bed every night.

When Alison woke up the next morning to let the dogs out, she reached for Bunny's harness—only to realize it had been cut again, this time in two places, in exactly the same manner that the first harness had been cut. To her added amazement, the cuts looked absolutely identical.

Alison was mystified. How had it happened? When she'd taken the harness off of Bunny the night before, it was perfectly fine. Who could possibly have gotten into the house and committed the malicious deed again? And why? Obviously, the phantom snipper wasn't interested in stealing Bunny, and even if he were, he didn't need to cut her harness to abduct her. What could be his—or her—motive?

Alison searched everywhere for the missing pieces of harness—outside, under the bed, around the couch, upstairs, and downstairs—with no luck. Could Bunny have possibly chewed her way out of the harness? She was a spirited girl who, if there had been any way at all, would have wiggled out of it. But no, Alison would have seen the evidence when she removed the harness, and there were no signs of gnawing or fraying. Besides, the cuts were on a part of the harness where Bunny couldn't reach.

Alison's roommate was equally stumped. Then she mentioned that she had heard banging downstairs in the middle of the night and had even locked the bedroom door.

That night, when Alison undid Bunny's harness, she carefully balled it up with Lexie's harness. The following morning, the harnesses were still where she had left them—but both had been cut and with a level of precision that only a sharp tool could accomplish.

As hard as she tried, Alison simply could not come up with any but a supernatural explanation for the eerie occurrences. It had to be a ghost or poltergeist, one of those prankster spirits that likes to make mischief for no good reason.

When Alison told her mother about the bizarre events, her mom was silent for a moment. Then she said, "You never met your grandmother. She died a few years before you were born."

"Grandmother Ruth?" Alison asked.

"Yes. Do you know what her nickname was?"

Alison shook her head.

"Bunny."

Alison was dumbfounded. She had never heard anyone in the family mention a Bunny.

"That's really weird," she said. "But what would that have to do with anything?"

"Your grandmother was famous for her quilts. She made the most beautiful patterns, and she had a favorite pair of shears that no one was ever allowed to touch. Those shears, she said, made the cleanest cuts in the county. They could slice through iron if they had to."

Alison got the proverbial cold chill. Was it possible that Grandma Bunny was trying to contact her in some way, through the dog that was her namesake?

The mystery was never solved, but the harness cutting stopped. Alison believes that Grandma Bunny succeeded in her mission, which was simply to introduce herself to the granddaughter she'd never had a chance to meet.

Bibliography

Books

Cohen, Daniel. *Dangerous Ghosts.* 1996, G .F. Putnam's Sons).

Crain, Mary Beth. *Haunted Christmas.* 2009, Globe Pequot Press.

O'Donnell, Elliott. *The Screaming Skull and Other Ghost Stories.* 1969, Taplinger Publishing Co.

Rainbolt, Dusty. *Ghost Cats: Human Encounters with Feline Spirits.* 2007, Globe Pequot Press.

Russell, Randy, and Janet Barnett. *Ghost Dogs of the South.* 2001, John F. Blair Publishers.

Schlosser, S. E. *Spooky Michigan.* 2007, Globe Pequot Press

Sharp, Harold. *Animals in the Spirit World.* 1966, Psychic Press Ltd.

Warren, Joshua. *Pet Ghosts: Animal Encounters from Beyond the Grave.* 2006, New Page Books.

Magazines

Dworin, Carolyn H. "What's Your Pooch Thinking?" *Newsweek,* July 21, 2010.

Websites

www.about.com

www.americanchronicle.com

www.castleofspirits.com

www.freewebs.com/spiritseekers1/staffordshireghoststories .htm

www.ghosthaunts.com

Bibliography

www.ghosttheory.com
www.globalpsychics.com
www.hotels.about.com
www.islandhotel-cedarkey.com/ghoststories.html
www.metro.uk/weird
www.nzghosts.com
www.real-british-ghosts.com
www.yourghoststories.com

About the Author

Mary Beth Crain is the author of *Haunted U.S. Battlefields* and *Haunted Christmas*, both published by Globe Pequot Press. Her other books include the *Los Angeles Times* best-selling memoir *A Widow, a Chihuahua, and Harry Truman* (HarperCollins) and *Guardian Angels* (Running Press). She lives in Hart, Michigan, with her 15-year-old Chihuahua, Truman; her angel cat, Junior Augustus; and her demon cat, Lincoln Aurelius.